Oggie Cooder

PARTY ANIMAL!

Oggie Cooder

PARTY ANIMAL!

sarah weeks

Illustrations by Doug Holgate

To Rowan!
[signature]
Weeks
2013

SCHOLASTIC INC.

New York Toronto London Auckland
Sydney Mexico City New Delhi Hong Kong

No part of this publication may be reproduced, stored in a
retrieval system, or transmitted in any form or by any means,
electronic, mechanical, photocopying, recording, or otherwise,
without written permission of the publisher. For information
regarding permission, write to Scholastic Inc., Attention:
Permissions Department, 557 Broadway, New York, NY 10012.

This book was originally published in hardcover
by Scholastic Press in 2009.

ISBN 978-0-439-92796-3

12 11 10 9 8 7 6 5 4 3 2   12 13 14 15 16/0

Printed in the U.S.A.   40
This edition first printing, July 2011

The text was set in Janson Text.
Book design by Elizabeth B. Parisi

For Pat Fedler and her beautiful New
granddaughter, Madison

1

Prrrrr-ip! Prrrrr-ip!

Oggie Cooder fluttered his tongue against the roof of his mouth. He always did that when he was excited about something.

"Check it out, Turk," he cried happily. "Look who just got invited to Donnica Perfecto's birthday party. *Can you believe it?*"

Oggie's dog, Turk, loved to eat paper. So when Oggie proudly held out the invitation he'd just received in the morning mail, Turk misunderstood and thought he was being offered a snack. In two quick bites the invitation disappeared.

"Hey!" Oggie laughed. "You were supposed to *read* it, not *eat* it!"

Turk, whose full name was Turkey-on-Rye (like the sandwich), burped and wagged his tail.

Oggie finished eating his breakfast and carried his empty cereal bowl over to the sink to rinse it out. Looking out the window, he saw Donnica Perfecto coming out of her house, her bubblegum-pink backpack slung over one shoulder. Mrs. Perfecto, in a long flowered bathrobe and hair curlers, followed after her daughter. She looked nervous.

"Don't worry, Cupcake!" she called. "Everything's going to be fine on Saturday. *Just fine.*" Then she blew a kiss and waved, but Donnica only glared at her and marched off.

Grabbing his own backpack, Oggie made a quick pit stop at the fridge for a few slices of processed American cheese, which he slipped into his back pocket for later. He gave Turk a good-bye pat on the head and raced out the door.

"Hey, Donnica! Wait up!" Oggie cried as he ran down the front steps.

Ever since his aunt Hettie had taught him how to crochet, Oggie had been making his own shoelaces. The night before, he'd crocheted himself a new pairing — orange and green, one of his favorite color combinations. Oggie thought they went nicely with the new blue-and-yellow-checked pants his mother had brought home from the store for him that week. Unfortunately one of the shoelaces was a little too long, and when the end of it caught on a loose nail on the steps, Oggie went tumbling head over heels into the bushes. Luckily he wasn't hurt, but by the time he pulled himself together, brushed the leaves out of his hair, and retied his shoelace in a double bow, Donnica had rounded the corner and was out of sight.

Oggie finally caught up with her in the schoolyard at Truman Elementary.

"I hope you don't mind," Oggie panted, holding his side and trying to catch his breath, "but I have about a *bazillion* questions I need to ask you."

"What's the matter with you, Oggie Cooder?" Donnica snarled as she spun around on her heel to face him. "Can't you see I'm having the worst day of my life?"

Now that she mentioned it, Oggie did notice that Donnica's eyebrows were scrunched down and bunched together in a knot over the top of her pointy little nose. And her shiny pink gloss-covered lips, which were usually turned up in a self-satisfied smirk, were pulled down at the corners in an unhappy pout.

Oggie hated to see people upset. Even Donnica Perfecto, who wasn't very nice to him.

"What's wrong?" he asked with genuine concern.

"You mean besides the fact that those pants you've got on are so hideous they're giving me a headache?" Donnica said.

"Maybe you should ask the school nurse for an aspirin," said Oggie. He didn't realize that Donnica's head wasn't really hurting, she was just making fun of his pants.

"Aspirin isn't going to fix what's wrong with my life," Donnica complained.

"What's wrong with your life?" Oggie asked,

surprised. It seemed to him Donnica Perfecto had a pretty great life. For one thing, she had a swimming pool in her backyard. When Oggie felt hot, the only way he had to cool off was to run through the sprinkler.

"I'll tell you what's wrong with my life," Donnica grumbled. "Because of my father and his stupid, boring old store, my whole birthday party is ruined."

Mr. Perfecto owned the largest appliance store in Wawatosa, Wisconsin. Walk into any house in town, chances were that the microwave in the kitchen and the television in the den had been purchased from Big Dealz. Any house, that is, except Oggie's. Mr. and Mrs. Cooder believed that microwave ovens and televisions — not to mention marshmallows, air fresheners, and milk sold in plastic jugs — were all bad for your brain cells.

"Are you planning to have your party at your dad's store?" asked Oggie, who hadn't had time to study the details of the invitation before Turk had eaten it.

Donnica heaved an exasperated sigh.

"Why would anybody have a birthday party in an appliance store?" she asked.

"I don't know." Oggie shrugged. "If I had a swimming pool like yours, I'd have my birthday party there."

The Perfectos lived directly across Tullahoma Street from the Cooders, and although Oggie had never been in their beautiful sky-blue kidney-shaped swimming pool, Turk had jumped in once, uninvited, after managing to get loose one day.

"*Obviously*, I'm going to have a pool party," said Donnica. "I *always* have a pool party. But I already told everybody that this year was going to be different. I told them there would be a big surprise. Who's going to want to come to a plain old ordinary pool party now?"

"I will!" cried Oggie, who had never been invited to any of Donnica's parties before.

Oggie undid the strings on his backpack and pulled out a plastic bag filled with dried apricots.

"Want one?" he asked Donnica.

"Ewww," she said, turning up her nose at the apricots. "They're *brown*."

"That's 'cause they're from the health food store. My mom says the orange ones you get at the grocery store have a ton of chemicals in them that can ruin your brain cells."

Donnica ignored him and went back to her whining.

"It's just not fair," she said. "Why does Daddy's big promotion for his store have to be on the same day as my party? Why didn't he listen to me when I told him what I wanted? It's my birthday. I'm supposed to get everything I want for my birthday. That's the rule."

This seemed like the perfect opportunity for Oggie to ask Donnica the most important of the *bazillion* questions he had for her.

"What do you want for your birthday?" he said.

"I want to get you something that you'll really, really like because I'm really, really happy that you invited me to your party. Actually, I'm not really, really happy. *Prrrrr-ip! Prrrrr-ip!* I'm more like really, really, *really* —"

"I get the point," Donnica interrupted. Oggie Cooder was more annoying than a broken fingernail.

The big red doors of Truman Elementary School swung open and students began filing into the building to begin the day.

"So anyway," said Oggie, trotting along next to Donnica as they started up the steps of the school, "can you think of something I could give you for your birthday?"

Donnica was about to tell Oggie to get lost and quit bothering her, when a lightbulb suddenly went on over her head. Actually there *was* something she wanted Oggie to give her for her birthday! Something Donnica had been wanting from the moment Mrs. Perfecto had made her write Oggie's name on one of her bubblegum-pink party invitations. Donnica wanted Oggie Cooder NOT to come to her party. And as anyone who knew her would tell you, Donnica Perfecto was really good at getting what she wanted.

Really, really, *really* good.

2

*O*ggie didn't have time to think about Donnica's birthday party anymore that morning. He had to work on a history report, which was due the following week. The topic he'd chosen for his report was famous inventors, which was no big surprise since Inventor was among the top ten things Oggie thought he might like to be when he grew up.

In the library, Oggie found a book called *Whose Idea Was It?* that looked promising. He sat down, opened it up to the table of contents, and began to run his finger down a list of famous inventors.

Alexander Graham Bell
George Washington Carver
Thomas Edison
Henry Ford

Benjamin Franklin

Samuel Morse

Elisha Otis

Oggie stopped.

"Who's Elisha Otis?" he wondered aloud. He flipped through the pages until he found the chapter describing how, in 1854, Elisha Otis had demonstrated the new elevator he had invented by ascending to a dizzying height in front of a crowd of people at a state fair and then having his assistant cut the ropes to prove that the brakes he had fashioned out of two wagon springs would keep the elevator from plummeting to the ground.

"Prrrrr-ip! Prrrrr-ip!" Oggie found that very exciting.

Donnica, who was sitting at a nearby table, gave Oggie a dirty look.

"Must you make that annoying sound?" she whined.

"I can't help it," Oggie told her excitedly. "I never knew who invented elevator brakes before."

"Shhh," said Ms. Hepper, the school librarian, pressing a long pale finger to her lips. "Do I need to remind you that the library is a quiet place, Oggie?"

"Sorry," Oggie whispered apologetically.

As Oggie turned the pages of the book, he was fascinated to learn about all kinds of interesting and important things people had invented over the years. Steam engines and telegraphs, ice-cream makers and electronic cow-milkers. The more he read, the more convinced he became that being an inventor would be a great profession for him. He hoped he could be like Elisha Otis and invent something as useful as elevator brakes.

At 11:45, Ms. Hepper announced to the students in the library that they had ten minutes left to finish up. Oggie carried his book over to the circulation desk to check it out.

"Necessity is the mother of invention," whispered Ms. Hepper with an approving nod as she ran the scanner over Oggie's book.

"Excuse me?" said Oggie.

"I believe it was Plato who said it," she told him.

Oggie had never heard of the great philosopher Plato. In fact, he'd misunderstood Ms. Hepper completely and thought that she had said "Plano," which was a town in Texas Oggie knew about because his uncle Vern had once ridden on a pig in a rodeo competition there.

"It means that the main reason things get invented is because people feel a need to have them," Ms. Hepper explained.

Oggie thought about that for a second and decided it made a lot of sense, though he wasn't sure what it had to do with Plano, Texas.

When he got back to his classroom, Oggie stashed his library book in his desk, grabbed his lunch, and headed down to the cafeteria, or — as some of the kids at Truman liked to call it — the *Barf-eteria*. Amy Schneider was waiting for Oggie when he got there.

"Who invented braces?" Oggie asked as he plopped himself down in his usual spot across the table from Amy.

Amy and Oggie were friends. Not boyfriend and girlfriend, just friends who happened to be a boy and a girl. Amy didn't mind that Oggie said *prrrrr-ip!* when he was excited about something, and Oggie didn't mind that Amy was shy and had a mouth so full of braces and rubber bands that it was sometimes hard to understand her when she spoke. Amy had to remove her rubber bands whenever she ate, and she was just finishing up the process when Oggie arrived.

"I don't know who invented braces," she said, dropping the last of the tiny green rubber bands onto the neat little pile she had made on her napkin. "But whoever it was must be rich. My parents told me that with all the money they've spent on straightening my teeth, they could have bought a brand-new car."

"I bet you could *make* a car out of all that metal in your mouth," said Oggie. "And you could use the rubber bands to make the tires."

Amy giggled and took a nice, big, rubber-band-free bite of her tuna fish sandwich.

Meanwhile, across the cafeteria at a round table in a prime spot near the window, Donnica Perfecto was about to deliver the bad news to her friends, Dawn and Hannah.

"My birthday party is going to be a disaster," she said. "And I'm talking a *total* disaster."

"I thought you told us there was going to be a big surprise," said Dawn.

"Yeah, remember you said it was going to be the biggest surprise ever?" Hannah reminded her.

"Well, it's not happening," Donnica reported.

"But you've been talking about it for weeks!" Hannah pressed. "You said this was going to be your best —"

"I know what I said," snapped Donnica. "But it's not happening. Read my lips: TOTAL DISASTER. Got it?"

"At least tell us what the surprise was going to be," Hannah said.

"Trust me. You don't want to know," Donnica replied as she pulled the lid off her Peachy-Keen-O-flavored yogurt, licked it, and then handed it to Hannah, who took it from her without a word.

Donnica Perfecto didn't "do" garbage. When she had something that needed to be thrown out, she simply handed it to Hannah or Dawn and they took care of it for her. Hannah took the sticky yogurt lid and placed it next to her own banana peel and crumpled napkin.

"Come on," Dawn begged. "Tell us what the surprise was going to be."

Donnica took a bite of yogurt, then set her spoon down.

"Okay," she finally agreed, "but don't say I didn't warn you. You're going to be totally bummed out when I tell you who was *almost* going to be the entertainment at my party."

Dawn and Hannah looked at Donnica expectantly.

"Tell us already," Hannah urged.

Donnica took a deep breath before answering — "*Cheddar Jam.*"

3

Dawn and Hannah were so stunned their mouths fell open in simultaneous shock.

"*Cheddar Jam?*" Hannah managed to croak.

"Are you saying what I think you're saying?" Dawn gasped in amazement. "Were they really going to play at your party?"

Donnica groaned and covered her face with both hands.

Cheddar Jam (a rock band named in honor of one of Wisconsin's most important contributions to the world — cheddar cheese) was made up of four *very* cute and *somewhat* musical local high school boys. They'd made quite a splash at Truman Elementary when they'd played at the Valentine Dance earlier that year.

"I told you you'd be bummed out," said Donnica.

"That's the understatement of the century," Hannah told her.

"Why aren't they coming?" Dawn asked.

"Because Daddy totally blew it," Donnica said bitterly. "He told me he was going to get somebody good to entertain at the store in the morning and then pay them extra to come over to my party afterward. So I told him to get Cheddar Jam. That's what I said — *'Daddy, get me Cheddar Jam'* — but did he listen?"

Donnica heaved a heavy sigh and picked up her spoon to take a bite of yogurt, but she changed her mind and pushed the plastic container toward Hannah, who added it to the throwaway pile. The girls were quiet for a minute and then Dawn asked —

"If Cheddar Jam isn't coming, who did your dad get instead?"

Donnica could barely bring herself to answer.

"Bumbles," she muttered through clenched teeth.

"*What?*" cried Hannah in disbelief.

"No way!" said Dawn.

"It's not my fault," Donnica said defensively. "I *told* my father to get Cheddar Jam. I can't help it if he got Bumbles the Juggling Bear instead."

"Why don't you do what you did when you wanted a new cell phone?" Dawn suggested.

"Yeah," said Hannah. "Pitch a fit and tell him if he doesn't give you what you want, you're not going to let him walk you down the aisle on your wedding day."

"Uh, *duh*. Don't you think I tried that already? He said it was too late. He already promised Bumbles the job. He said Bumbles told him he's broke and needs the work." Donnica groaned and put her head in her hands again.

Over on the other side of the room, Oggie Cooder had somehow managed to spill an entire carton of chocolate milk on the floor. He'd tried to use his sandwich as a sponge to soak up the milk, but that had only made matters worse. On his way over to the lunch counter to get some paper napkins to clean up the mess, he passed near Donnica's table and figured he'd take the opportunity to ask another of his *bazillion* important questions about her birthday party.

"Hey, Donnica?" he called to her. "Is it okay if I wear my bathing suit over to your house on Saturday, or should I bring it with me and change into it when I get there?"

For the second time that day, Dawn's and Hannah's mouths dropped open in simultaneous shock. Had Donnica actually invited *Oggie Cooder* to her birthday party?

"I know what you're thinking," Donnica told them. "But it wasn't *my* idea."

It was Donnica's mother who had insisted that Oggie be invited to the party.

"I want you to send an invitation to the Cooder boy across the street," Mrs. Perfecto had announced one morning as Donnica sat at the table carefully addressing the envelopes for her party invitations.

"You must be joking, Mother. Why would I do that?" asked Donnica.

"He's our neighbor, Cupcake."

"So what? He plays with cheese and makes that annoying sound with his tongue all the time. Plus he dresses like he's from another planet. Yesterday he wore a bow tie to school. *A bow tie*, Mother."

"I admit he's a bit odd," Mrs. Perfecto had said. "But the Wawatosa Gardening Club is considering me for membership."

"So?" said Donnica, running the tip of her pointy tongue along an envelope flap before adding it to the pile to be stamped.

"I've wanted to be in that club for years. Everyone who's anyone is in it," Mrs. Perfecto explained.

"Why don't you just join if you want to be in it so badly?"

"It's not that easy. You have to be invited. The board of directors comes and examines your land-scaping before they'll even consider you for membership."

"What's landscaping?" asked Donnica, licking another flap and tossing the envelope onto the pile.

"Flowers and bushes," said Mrs. Perfecto.

"We have plenty of flowers and bushes," Donnica pointed out.

"Yes, but they're all droopy and sad-looking," said Mrs. Perfecto. "That is, they were until Isabel Cooder stepped in. Ever since she showed me how to put crushed eggshells around my plants to keep away the slugs, my begonias have been blooming like there's no tomorrow."

"Hello? What do eggshells have to do with inviting Oggie Cooder to my birthday party?" Donnica asked.

"I need to stay on Isabel Cooder's good side. She's my only hope of getting into the club."

"*Mother*," Donnica whined, "Oggie Cooder is the dweebiest dweeb to ever walk the earth. I'll *die* of embarrassment if he comes to my birthday party."

But Mrs. Perfecto's mind was made up. She stood over Donnica as she wrote Oggie's name on one of the pink envelopes. Then, to make sure that Donnica didn't "accidentally" forget to mail it, Mrs. Perfecto carried the invitation down to the corner and dropped it into the mailbox herself.

If Mrs. Perfecto thought that the battle was over and she had won, then clearly she had forgotten who she was dealing with.

"You're joking, right?" said Hannah. "You didn't really invite Oggie Cooder to your party, did you?"

Donnica reached into her pocket and pulled out her pink lip gloss.

"I invited him," she said, pausing for a minute to slowly run the shiny gloss over her lips. "But trust me, he's not going to come."

4

Lunch hour was over. Hannah took care of throwing out the trash, then she and Dawn took up their usual positions on either side of Donnica, and the trio exited the Barf-eteria together. Amy Schneider and Oggie Cooder were in the same fourth-grade class as Donnica Perfecto and her friends, so they headed down the hall in the same direction toward Mr. Snolinovsky's classroom. At the beginning of the year Oggie had found it difficult to remember how to pronounce his teacher's name correctly. *SNOW-LINN-OFF-SKEE* was much harder to say than the names of any of his other teachers had been.

That afternoon in class, Oggie couldn't seem

to stop *prrrrr-ip-ing*. Mr. Snolinovsky spoke to him about it several times, but even so, Oggie *prrrrr-ip-ed* in the middle of math and twice during science. He was so excited about having been invited to Donnica's birthday party he simply couldn't contain himself. Oggie had always wondered what it would be like to swim in the Perfectos' pool, and now at last he was going to find out.

The last hour of every school day, Mr. Snolinovsky's class did creative writing. At the beginning of the year, Oggie had worried that he wouldn't be able to think of anything interesting to write about. But once Mr. Snolinovsky had explained to him that stories were like seeds, and that Oggie was like a watermelon, loaded with seeds, Creative Writing had become his favorite subject. During the hour, Mr. Snolinovsky liked to walk around the room, peering over people's shoulders to see what they were working on.

"Fascinating," he said that day as he looked at the story Bethie Hudson was writing about her goldfish, Honeymoon.

"Exciting," he said as he read the paragraph David Korben had just finished about a slam-dunk contest he'd been in at basketball camp.

"Hmmm," he said as he bent down and squinted hard at Oggie's paper. "Does that sentence say 'Uncle Worm was from Switzerland'?"

Oggie had terrible handwriting, so it was no surprise that Mr. Snolinovsky was having trouble reading what he had written.

"No. It says, 'Uncle Vern won the Stinkerama,'" Oggie explained. "It's an armpit contest they have every year at the Zanesville County Fair. My uncle is the champion. He can play 'Yankee Doodle' with his hand under his arm, *and* his pits have been voted the stinkiest in the county for three years straight."

"Impressive," said Mr. Snolinovsky, stroking his mustache.

"That's nothing," Oggie told him. "You should see Uncle Vern chunk a mini-pumpkin. He made this catapult thing out of some old underwear elastic and a pair of chopsticks and, man oh man, he can make those babies fly. They have a contest for that in Zanesville, too."

Mr. Snolinovsky laughed. His name might have been difficult to pronounce, but he was the first teacher Oggie had ever had who not only accepted Oggie for who he was, but seemed to genuinely like him.

When Creative Writing was over, everybody put their stories away and Mr. Snolinovsky wrote the homework assignment for that night on the board. There was a page of math problems to solve in the workbook, a spelling test to prepare for, and, at the bottom of the list, a strange word Oggie had never seen before — *HAIKU.*

"What's *hay-cue?*" asked America Johnson, leaning forward in her seat as she squinted at the blackboard.

"It's pronounced *high-coo,* and it's a kind of Japanese poem," Mr. Snolinovsky explained.

There was an unhappy grumble from the class, especially the boys.

"Poetry stinks," groaned Jackson Polito.

"I'm down with that," agreed David Korben, who was interested in only one thing in life — basketball.

"You like math, don't you, Jackson?" Mr. Snolinovsky asked.

"Sure. Math is about numbers. Numbers are cool. Poetry is about mushy feelings and butterflies and other *un*-cool junk like that," Jackson said.

"What would you say if I told you that haiku is a kind of poetry that uses numbers?" asked Mr. Snolinovsky.

"Poems about numbers?" said Dylan James, who hardly ever talked in class. Dylan had thick, blond hair, which he had a habit of smoothing back with both hands. Oggie had heard that his family had moved to Wawatosa from Chicago over the summer.

Bethie Hudson waved her hand in the air excitedly.

"Listen to what I just made up!" she said when Mr. Snolinovsky called on her. "'Roses are red, violets are blue, two times eleven is twenty-two.'"

Mr. Snolinovsky smiled.

"Very nice," he said. "And I'm delighted to see you've been working on your times tables, Bethie. But when you write haiku, the only numbers you have to be concerned with are five, seven, and five."

"Don't tell me you're going to make us write five hundred and seventy-five words!" Jackson cried in horror.

"Don't worry," said Mr. Snolinovsky. "A haiku is a very short poem. It doesn't rhyme and it's only three lines long."

"Yes!" cried Jackson.

"So what do the two fives and the seven have to do with anything?" asked America.

"You use those numbers to count the syllables in your poem," Mr. Snolinovsky explained.

"You mean the poem only has to have sixteen syllables?" asked David, whose strongest subject was obviously not math.

"Seventeen," corrected Mr. Snolinovsky. "And, yes, that's how many syllables the poem has to have.

Five in the first line, seven in the second, and five in the third line."

"Do the words have to be in Japanese?" asked Donnica. "Because the only Japanese word I know is 'sushi,' and I am *not* writing a poem about raw fish."

Mr. Snolinovsky assured everyone that he did not expect the poems to be written in Japanese. Then he read a few examples from a book of haiku. The one that Oggie liked best was about a dog waiting for its owner to return home.

Friend beside the door
Ears up, head cocked, he listens
Eager for footsteps

Turk was always very happy to see Oggie when he got home. And he was usually waiting right at the door when Oggie got there. Oggie wondered whether that was because Turk was listening for his footsteps like the dog in the poem.

"I want each of you to write a haiku tonight and bring it in to class tomorrow," said Mr. Snolinovsky. "We're going to do something with them that I think you'll find very interesting,"

Actually, most of the kids in the class would find it interesting. But for one person — a certain individual sitting in the first seat of the third row in Mr. Snolinovsky's fourth grade classroom — the experience was going to be absolutely *shocking*.

5

Amy raised her hand.

"What are our haikus supposed to be about?" she asked.

"Before I answer that, Amy, let me point out that the plural of 'haiku' is 'haiku,' not 'haikus,'" said Mr. Snolinovsky. "And I want the haiku to be about you."

"Gross, we gotta write a poem about *Amy*? What if we don't want to write about *a girl*?" moaned Jonathan Bass, who had five sisters at home, which was five too many as far as he was concerned.

Mr. Snolinovsky laughed. "What I meant, Jon, is that I want each of you to write a haiku that tells us who you are."

Jackson was counting on his fingers.

"Awesome!" he shouted. "I've got my first and last lines already: *Jackson Polito*. Pretty lucky to have a name with five syllables, huh?"

"Mine, too!" cried Hannah Hummerman excitedly.

"Hang on," said Mr. Snolinovsky. "In order for us to do what I have in mind, you may not use your names in your haiku."

"No fair!" cried Jackson.

"Yeah," agreed David Korben, who hadn't counted carefully enough and thought that his name had five syllables, too.

"In addition to keeping your names out of the poems, I also don't want you to put your names on your papers," Mr. Snolinovsky went on.

"How are you going to know whose is whose?" asked America.

"That's where the challenge lies. If your haiku contains the *essence* of who you are, then it should be obvious who wrote it."

"What do you mean by 'essence'?" David asked.

"I think it has something to do with shampoo," Dawn said.

"I thought 'essence' meant something smelly," said Jonathan.

"Like Uncle Vern's armpits, you mean?" Oggie asked.

Donnica rolled her eyes. Oggie Cooder was *so* annoying. If he wasn't *prrrrr-ip-ing* all over the place or wearing bow ties, he was talking about his strange relatives in Ohio. There was no way, NO WAY he was coming to her birthday party. She was definitely going to see to that.

"Jonathan is right — 'essence' can mean smelly in some instances," Mr. Snolinovsky explained to the class, "but in this case it means something else." He pulled one of the classroom dictionaries off the shelf, turned to *E*, and read the definition: "Essence: the choicest or most important part of an idea, experience, or person." He slid the dictionary back into its place on the shelf and turned to the class. "I want your haiku to be about the choicest, most important part of what makes you who you are."

A few minutes later, as the class lined up at the door for dismissal, Donnica wasn't thinking about the essence of who she was. Instead, she was demonstrating it.

"How could Daddy possibly think that I would want a juggling bear at my party?" she whined to her friends. "Juggling bears are for babies. Do I look like a baby? I mean, *really*. A juggling bear? Puh —"

"— leeze." Dawn and Hannah automatically finished Donnica's word for her.

Following an argument they'd had with Donnica earlier in the year, Dawn and Hannah had threatened to stop finishing her words for her. But the habit had proved too difficult to break.

As they left the classroom and started down the hall, Oggie and Amy, who were walking next to each other, got close enough to be able to overhear the tail end of what Donnica was saying.

"How could this be happening to me?" she said. "Bumbles the Bear at *my* birthday party."

As soon as Oggie heard that, he let loose a particularly enthusiastic *prrrrr-ip!*

Donnica cringed at the sound.

Oggie had seen Bumbles many times, juggling at the farmers' market on Sunday mornings. Bumbles wasn't a real bear — he was a person dressed up in a fur suit who juggled bowling pins and fruit and other assorted objects in hopes that the people who stopped to watch would toss coins or, better yet, dollar bills into the battered black top hat he set out on the sidewalk. Oggie loved to watch Bumbles. He was funny and even though he sometimes pretended to drop things, that was just part of the act. He was actually a very good juggler.

"*Prrrrr-ip! Prrrrr-ip!* First you invite me to your party, and now I find out that Bumbles is going to be there, too?! I can't believe it!" Oggie exclaimed happily.

"Me neither," grumbled Donnica.

Everybody was so busy thinking about Donnica's birthday party that nobody was paying any attention to Amy Schneider. If they had been, they would have noticed that she suddenly looked terribly uncomfortable.

"I'll see you tomorrow," she told Oggie, then hurried off down the hall.

Oggie stopped to get a drink of water at the drinking fountain while Donnica and her friends continued walking.

"Do you realize this could ruin my reputation?" Donnica said glumly.

Dawn shot a quick look at Hannah. Donnica was their friend, but her reputation wasn't exactly something to be proud of, unless you happened to think that being bossy, mean, and completely self-centered was a *good* thing.

"Just think, if Cheddar Jam had come to your party, I would have gotten to meet J.J. in person." Hannah sighed. "Maybe he would have even come over and talked to me. I one-hundred-percent guarantee that if that ever happened I would totally faint from happiness." She put the back of her hand up to her forehead dramatically and fell over sideways onto Dawn's shoulder in a fake faint.

J.J. was the lead singer for Cheddar Jam. Like the other three boys in the band, he was a senior at Wawatosa High School. At the Valentine Dance, Hannah had spent the entire time staring at him. She was crazy about the way his long hair fell into his eyes when he was singing.

"How can you be thinking about yourself at a time like this? *Hello?* I'm having a crisis here, in case you haven't noticed," Donnica complained. But Hannah seemed not to have heard her.

"If only your dad had hired Cheddar Jam," Hannah continued dreamily, "that would have been in —"

" — credible," said Dawn, finishing the word for her.

"Hey!" Donnica said, stamping her foot. "How many times do I have to tell you two? *I* do the first syllables around here. That's the rule."

"Sorry," Hannah apologized. "I was distracted." Then she put the back of her hand to her forehead again. "I can't stop thinking about J.J. — I'm telling you, if I ever get to meet him in person I one-hundred-percent guarantee —"

Donnica reached over and snatched Hannah's hand away from her forehead.

"I one-hundred-percent guarantee I'm going to strangle you if you don't stop saying that," she growled. "Don't you realize how humiliating this experience is going to be for me? There's a juggling bear coming to my birthday party."

"I have an idea," Hannah offered in an attempt to get back on Donnica's good side. "Since the party is going to be *outside*, why don't you tell Bumbles he's only allowed to juggle *inside*. That way nobody will even know he's there."

"You know, that's not a bad idea," Donnica said, brightening a little.

Hannah smiled, feeling very pleased with herself.

"Maybe you could do the same thing with Oggie," she suggested.

"Oh, don't worry about him," Donnica said. "I already came up with a plan for how to deal with Oggie Cooder. I'm just waiting for the right time to put it into action."

And that right time happened to be right around the corner.

6

Oggie walked home alone that afternoon. On the way he passed a repair truck from the phone company. Two men — one tall and thin, the other short and squat — were standing on the ground pointing up at the telephone wires that ran high overhead. Then the short man climbed into a large white metal box attached to a long pole on the back of the truck. A second later the box began to rise up into the air until the man was close enough to the wires to be able to reach them.

"Do you mind if I ask you what that thing is called?" Oggie asked the worker who was still standing on the ground.

"It's called a cherry picker."

Oggie laughed. "That's a funny name," he said.

"Maybe so, but it sure beats climbing a ladder, which is what we used to have to do before this thing was invented," the man replied.

"Necessity is the mother of invention," said Oggie, suddenly remembering Ms. Hepper's words.

"Did you make that up?" asked the man.

"No, some guy in Texas did," Oggie told him.

As Oggie watched the man in the cherry picker working on the wires overhead, he absentmindedly reached into his back pocket and pulled out one of the slices of processed American cheese he'd been carrying around all day. Oggie always kept a few slices of cheese in his pocket in case he felt like charving. "Charving" is a combination of the words "chewing" and "carving," and Oggie could charve cheese into the shape of just about anything he wanted. It was one of his favorite hobbies.

"What the heck are you doing with that cheese, son?" asked the worker, giving Oggie a funny look.

"Oh." Oggie held up the cheese to show the man. "I was charving your cherry picker. See?"

The man's eyes suddenly lit up with recognition. "You're that boy who was all over the newspapers a while back, aren't you? The one who was almost on that TV show." He looked at the cheese, pointed, and laughed. "Well, I'll be. That's my buddy in the bucket right there, isn't it?"

Oggie smiled and nodded. For a brief time he'd been sort of famous in Wawatosa because he'd been invited to charve on a TV show called *Hidden Talents*. In the end, though, he'd decided he wasn't cut out for Hollywood.

"Okay, George!" called the man who was up high working on the wires. "Bring 'er down."

While George worked the controls to bring his friend safely back down to the ground, Oggie asked him if he knew who had invented the cherry picker. George said he didn't, and then he asked his friend, whose name it turned out was also George.

"Nope," said the short George as he climbed out

of the bucket. "But who cares who invented it, as long as it works?"

George and George asked if they could keep the charved cherry picker Oggie had made so they could take it home to show to their kids. Oggie quickly charved a second cherry picker so they could each have one, then he left the two men admiring his cheesy handiwork and walked the rest of the way home trying to imagine what it would feel like to invent something as useful as a cherry picker.

As usual, Turk was waiting at the door when Oggie got home.

"Were you listening for my footsteps, boy?" Oggie asked as he crouched down next to Turk to give him a good belly scratch. Turk burped and rolled over onto his back, closing his eyes and wagging his tail with pleasure.

Every day after school, Oggie took Turk for a long walk. Sometimes they went to the park where Oggie would throw tennis balls for Turk to chase.

Other times they'd walk into town and drop in at Too Good to Be Threw, the resale shop that Oggie's parents owned and ran in downtown Wawatosa.

Turk knew the way to the park by heart and he knew the way to the store, too, but this time he didn't choose to go in either of those directions. Instead he pulled Oggie down the street and around the corner toward Walnut Acres, a new housing development that had sprung up in the last year or so. Oggie had never walked around there before. He thought that Walnut Acres sounded like the kind of place a squirrel might want to live.

Turk stopped to sniff at a bush in front of a house with a yellow door and a brand-new bike parked in the driveway. A boy in a red-and-white-striped shirt was leaning over, using a pump to put air in the front tire. His back was to Oggie, but when he stood up and turned around, Oggie was surprised to see who it was.

"Hi, Dylan," called Oggie. "I didn't know you lived in Walnut Acres."

"Yeah," Dylan answered. He raised his arms and smoothed his hair back with both hands, then pointed at Turk and said, "Cool dog."

Oggie walked up the driveway in order to properly introduce Turk to Dylan.

"His real name is Turkey-on-Rye," Oggie explained, "but I call him Turk for short."

Dylan bent down and scratched Turk behind the ears. In return, he got a big slobbery dog kiss on the cheek.

"Have you done your homework yet?" Oggie asked Dylan.

"Nope."

"Have you figured out what your haiku's going to be about yet?"

"Nope."

Oggie noticed something pink sticking out of Dylan's back pocket and knew right away what it was. "Are you going to Donnica's birthday party, too?" he asked.

Dylan smoothed back his hair again.

"Nope," he said. "I don't like girls."

"*Any* girls?" asked Oggie.

"Nope," Dylan replied. Then he pointed at Oggie's right foot. "Your shoe's untied."

Oggie looked down and saw that once again his right shoelace had come undone. He was going to have to measure more carefully from now on when he made his laces. Oggie looked around for a place to sit down and noticed a large red trunk sitting on the grass beside the driveway.

"Okay if I sit on this while I tie my shoe?" Oggie asked.

"Sure," said Dylan, smoothing his hair back again even though it hadn't moved a bit since the last time he'd done it.

If only Oggie had opened the lid of the red trunk instead of sitting down on it, everything might have been different. Instead he finished tying his shoelace in a triple knot, which he hoped would keep it tied once and for all. Then he stood up and walked over to Dylan, who had gone back to pumping up his bike tires.

"How about showing me your room?" Oggie said.

Dylan shrugged. "Okay."

Oggie followed Dylan into the house, leaving the red trunk and its very interesting contents behind.

7

Dylan's house was nice inside. Oggie met his mom, and she offered him a cookie.

"It doesn't have any marshmallows in it, does it?" asked Oggie.

"Are you allergic to marshmallows, Oggie?" Mrs. James seemed concerned.

"No, but I can't afford to lose any brain cells today," he explained. "I have to write a haiku later and I have a feeling it's going to be hard."

On the way up the stairs to Dylan's room, Oggie asked Dylan what he liked to do for fun.

"I'm into computers," Dylan told him. "Games and Googling stuff for fun, you know?"

Actually, Oggie didn't know. Computers were on

the list of things that his parents considered hazardous to his brain cells, so there was no Googling for fun at the Cooder house.

"Do you have any cards?" asked Oggie.

Dylan's face immediately lit up.

"You like cards?"

"You betcha," Oggie said enthusiastically. "I know a couple of good tricks I can teach you. Or we could play Old Maid. Or War."

Dylan's face fell. Oggie was obviously not thinking of the same kind of cards he was. In Chicago, Dylan's best friend had been named Bo. They'd done everything together. But since the James family had moved to Wawatosa, Dylan hadn't met anybody like Bo. Mostly he'd just been hanging around by himself, or tagging along after his older brother, Justin, when Justin wasn't too busy working.

Up in Dylan's room, Oggie learned that the cards Dylan was interested in weren't playing cards. They were called Ghouler cards, and Dylan collected them.

"I've got four hundred thirty-seven Ghorks, plus two of the four Shadow Zwills," Dylan told him proudly.

Oggie didn't have any idea what Ghorks or Shadow Zwills were, and he didn't see the point of collecting cards that you couldn't even play Old Maid with. He was, however, interested in the poster over Dylan's bed.

"Have you been to Hawaii?" he asked, admiring the picture of palm trees lining a black sandy beach.

"Yeah," said Dylan.

"I almost got a free trip to Hawaii once," Oggie told him. "I entered a contest. But I didn't win."

"Do you enter a lot of contests?" asked Dylan.

"Bazillions," said Oggie.

"Have you ever won anything?"

"Not yet. But next week I'm going to enter a birdcalling contest. I'm doing a yellow-bellied sapsucker. Want to hear?"

"Maybe later," said Dylan.

There was an awkward silence. Finally, to make conversation, Dylan said, "We went to Hawaii last Christmas. That's where I got the poster."

"My family always goes to Zanesville for Christmas," Oggie told him. "My uncle Vern can gargle 'Jingle Bells' with a mouth full of eggnog."

Dylan tried not to be too obvious about it as he snuck a quick peek at his watch. Oggie was nice, but Dylan didn't feel they had anything in common.

Downstairs a door slammed loudly.

"Yo, Little Bro!" called a deep voice.

"Up here!" yelled Dylan.

Oggie heard footsteps running up the stairs, and a minute later Dylan's older brother, Justin, opened the door. The two brothers looked a lot alike except that Justin was taller and his hair was much longer than Dylan's.

"I've gotta take my suit downtown to the cleaners. Can I borrow your bike?" Justin asked.

"Sure," Dylan said.

Justin looked at Oggie and whistled.

"Where'd you get those checkered pants, man? They're sweet."

"They're from my parents' store," Oggie told him.

"I didn't think this town had any stores that sold decent stuff like that," said Justin.

Oggie was proud of what his parents did for a living. "It's called Too Good to Be Threw," he said. "I get all my clothes from there. Except for my shoelaces. I make those myself."

Turk began to bark. Oggie had left him tied up outside because the James family had a cat. Turk felt the same way about cats as he did about paper, loose change, and dirty socks — *yum*.

"Okay, Turkey Boy, I get the message!" Oggie called out the window. Then he turned to Dylan and said, "I guess I should get going."

"Yeah," said Dylan, who still wished he could find somebody at Truman who at least knew what Ghouler cards were.

"I'd love to check out your parents' store," said

Justin, still admiring Oggie's pants. "I could really use a pair of those. But I'm so swamped I don't have any time to go shopping. I've got three jobs this weekend, plus I'm busing tables at the Clam Digger every night this week. I need all the work I can get. I'm saving up for a car."

"Tell Oggie what happened at the Clam Digger last night," Dylan said.

"Oh, some guy choked on a clam shell and I had to do the Heimlich maneuver on him."

"What's the Heimlich maneuver?" asked Oggie.

Justin put his arms around Dylan's middle to demonstrate.

"You put your fists together in the front like this, squeeze hard, and then watch out, because whatever the person's choking on comes flying out like a rocket."

"Neat-o!" said Oggie.

"Not as neat-o as those checkered pants you've got on, little dude," said Justin.

"If you want, I can ask my mom if she has any more like these at the store. If she does, I could bring them to you," Oggie offered. "What size do you wear?"

Justin told Oggie what size he wore and thanked him.

"I owe you one, man," he said.

Little did he know how soon he would be repaying the favor.

8

On his way out, Oggie stopped to say good-bye to Mrs. James and to thank her for the cookie.

"I hope you'll come visit Dylan again," she said with a smile. "He could use a nice friend like you. We bought him that bike hoping he'd ride around the neighborhood and explore a little, but all he seems to want to do is stay up in his room on the computer."

On the way home Oggie decided to practice his yellow-bellied sapsucker call. His interest in bird-calling had begun when his aunt Hettie sent him something called a Swiss Warbler. It was a small leather half-moon-shaped device that you put on your tongue. There was a tiny piece of cellophane on one side of it, and if you hissed air across it in just the right way, you could make very realistic-sounding chirps and twitters.

The yellow-bellied sapsucker has three different calls: *KWEE-URK kwee-urk*, which means "stay away from me," *week-week wurp-wurp*, which means "I like you," and *k-waan k-waan*, which means "I'm very excited."

As he turned the corner and started up Tullahoma Street, Oggie was concentrating hard on his *kwee-urk*. Mrs. Perfecto, who was standing out on her front lawn, staring at the bushes growing in front of her house, heard the strange sound and, seeing that it was Oggie, waved him over.

"Is your mother at home?" she asked anxiously.

"*Shleeze shill esh ush shorsh*," said Oggie, forgetting that he still had the Swiss Warbler in his mouth. Realizing his mistake, he quickly pulled it out and repeated his response. "She's still at the store."

"Oh," said Mrs. Perfecto, nervously eyeing the spitty Swiss Warbler in Oggie's hand. "Perhaps I'll give her a call later and see if she can stop by."

Turk started tugging on his leash. He was clearly interested in sniffing the Perfectos' bushes, but Oggie thought that might not be a great idea, especially with Mrs. Perfecto standing right there. He popped the Swiss Warbler back in his mouth so that he'd have both hands free to keep Turk on the sidewalk.

Mrs. Perfecto looked over at her bushes again and sighed. She was very worried. The Garden Club committee could stop by without warning at any time to inspect her yard. It just wouldn't do to have raggedy rhododendrons. She needed Isabel Cooder's help, and there wasn't a minute to spare.

Turning back to Oggie, Mrs. Perfecto smiled. "By the way," she said, a little more sweetly than was necessary, "did you receive the invitation to Donnica's party? I do hope your mother is aware that you've been invited, dear."

At the mention of Donnica's birthday party,

Oggie attempted to *prrrrr-ip!* But because of the Swiss Warbler in his mouth, it came out sounding more like a squawk.

Mrs. Perfecto was so startled by the sound that she put her hand to her heart.

"Oh, my!" she exclaimed.

Oggie pulled the spitty warbler out of his mouth once more.

"I wouldn't miss the party for anything," he told Mrs. Perfecto happily. "But I do have a question I need to ask Donnica. Is she home by any chance?"

"Why, yes. She's upstairs with her friends. Just a second and I'll get her for you." Mrs. Perfecto lifted her head and yelled at the top of her lungs, "DONNICA!"

A few seconds later an upstairs window slid open and Donnica stuck her head out.

Oggie waved up at her.

"Ewww," said Donnica, wrinkling her nose in disgust. "What are you doing here?"

"Mind your manners," scolded Mrs. Perfecto quickly. She couldn't afford to have her daughter being rude to Isabel Cooder's son — not with her rhododendrons looking the way they did. "Be polite, Cupcake. Our wonderful little neighbor here has something he needs to ask you."

"I was just wondering if you figured out yet what you want me to get you for your birthday," Oggie called up.

"Isn't that lovely?" cried Mrs. Perfecto.

Donnica's blue eyes narrowed slightly, like a cat preparing to pounce on a mouse. This was the moment she'd been waiting for.

"Come on up," she called down to Oggie in the same overly sweet voice her mother had just been using.

Knowing she only had a short time before Oggie got to her room, Donnica quickly pulled her head inside and closed the window. Then she turned to Dawn and Hannah, who were sitting next to each other on the big pink canopy bed.

"Remember that little plan I told you about?" she asked them. "Well, get ready because the time has come to put it into action."

"What do you want us to do?" asked Hannah.

"Nothing. Just leave the talking to me."

Oggie had never been inside the Perfectos' house before, but Mrs. Perfecto told him to go up the stairs and that Donnica's room would be the third door on the left.

"Can I bring my dog in with me?" he asked.

Mrs. Perfecto shuddered at the thought of a giant, hairy dog walking around on her nice clean carpets, but then she glanced at her raggedy rhododendrons and reconsidered.

"The Cooders are *all* welcome in our home," Mrs. Perfecto told him, quickly adding, "Make sure to tell your mother that I said that, won't you, dear?"

When Oggie reached the top of the stairs, he turned left and began to count. The first door he passed was the bathroom. Next to it was a narrow door that looked like some kind of a closet. The third door was closed and had a pink heart with a letter *D* painted on it.

Oggie knocked and Donnica told him to come in. As he opened the door and stepped inside, he tripped over the end of that pesky right shoelace, which had come undone again despite the triple knot. Oggie did his best to regain his balance, flapping his arms like a giant albatross, but despite his efforts, he ended up sprawled on Donnica's fuzzy pink rug with his head resting on the toe of her right shoe.

Donnica quickly pulled her foot out from under Oggie's head, letting it smoosh into the carpet. Oggie sat up and began to retie his shoelace — this time in a quadruple knot — while Turk made himself at home, sniffing around the room for a minute before settling down next to Oggie on the rug.

Donnica flashed Hannah and Dawn a watch-this kind of a look.

"Oggie" she began, "I think we need to have a little talk."

"Okay," Oggie said, smiling up at her.

"See, there's something you should know about my birthday party."

"*Prrrrr-ip! Prrrrr-ip!*" went Oggie. He couldn't help it. Every time the subject of the party came up, he felt happy all over again.

"Is there something you want to tell me about your present?" Oggie asked. "'Cause I want to get you something you really, really —"

"No!" Donnica put up a hand to stop him. "This is not about my present." She paused to sit down on the bed between Hannah and Dawn, who quickly scooted over to make room for her. "I want to talk to you about the B.P.R.'s."

"B.P.R.'s?" said Oggie.

"Birthday Party Rules," Donnica explained.

"You never had rules at any of your birthday parties before," blurted Dawn, forgetting the instruction she'd been given to keep quiet.

Donnica immediately jammed her elbow into Dawn's ribs hard enough to make her jump.

"Of course I did. You remember the rules, *don't you, Dawn?*" Donnica said pointedly.

"I do now," Dawn muttered, rubbing her tender ribs.

"Anyway," Donnica continued, turning her attention back to Oggie, "I thought I'd better tell you about the rules ahead of time since this is the first time you've ever come to one of my parties."

"All right," Oggie agreed.

But the truth was, as Dawn had said, there had never been any birthday party rules before. Donnica's big plan was to invent a bunch of rules she knew it would be impossible for Oggie to follow.

"If you can't follow the rules, you can't come to my party," she informed Oggie.

"Okay," he said. He'd never heard of birthday party rules before, but was certainly willing to do whatever it took in order to be allowed to come to Donnica's party and swim in her pool.

"Are you ready for Rule Number One?" Donnica asked Oggie.

"Ready," he told her.

Donnica held up a pink-glitter-polish-tipped finger. "NO *prrrrr-ip-ing* ALLOWED."

9

Donnica was delighted to see the worried look on Oggie's face. Her plan was working already!

"No *prrrrr-ip-ing*?" Oggie asked. "Gee, that might be kind of hard. See, I don't do it on purpose, it just pops out accidentally when I'm feeling happy."

"Well, it's not allowed to pop out at my party," said Donnica, folding her arms across her chest. "So if you can't control it, you can't come."

Oggie couldn't bear the thought of missing Donnica's party. There had to be something he could do to keep from *prrrrr-ip-ing* while he was there. When he got the hiccups he always held his breath or put sugar under his tongue. Maybe that would work. Or maybe if he *prrrrr-ip-ed* a whole bunch right before the party, he'd be all *prrrrr-ip-ed* out when he got there.

"I'll figure something out," Oggie told Donnica. "Is that the only rule?"

Donnica shook her head and put up a second finger.

"Rule Number Two: NO CROCHETED SHOE-LACES ALLOWED."

Oggie looked down at his feet. The quadruple knot he'd tied was still holding tight.

"I don't have any regular shoelaces," he said. "But I guess I could buy some, or maybe I could just wear slippers. I've got a pair of really nice fuzzy ones. They've got pom-poms on the toes. Are pom-poms allowed?"

Oggie's parents' store specialized in used clothing of all kinds. "Vintage," his mother called it. Donnica knew that almost everything in Oggie's wardrobe came from the store, which is why she was ready with Rule Number Three.

"NO USED CLOTHES ALLOWED," she

said. "And in case you're wondering, that includes bathing suits."

Instead of being upset by this, Oggie broke into a huge grin.

"No prob-lemio with the bathing suit-io!" he cried happily. "My mom just bought me a pair of swim trunks on sale at Selznick's department store. They're red with pineapples on them and they've even got pockets. And if I can't figure out what to wear on my feet I can always just come barefoot."

The plan was not working quite as well as Donnica had hoped, but she was not ready to give up yet. She was determined to keep Oggie Cooder away from her birthday party, no matter how many rules she had to come up with.

"Sorry," she said, holding up a fourth glitter-tipped finger. "Rule Number Four: NO RED BATHING SUITS ALLOWED."

"Really?" said Hannah, who had gotten so caught up in Donnica's rules, she'd forgotten they weren't real. She was worried about the fact that the bathing suit she was planning to wear to the party was also red. One sharp look from Donnica brought her quickly back to her senses just in time to save herself from a painful jab in the ribs.

"How many rules are there?" asked Oggie.

As many as it takes, thought Donnica, and she began to tick things off on her fingers.

"No tripping over your feet, no cheese charving, no talking about boring inventions, no Uncle Vern stories, no dorky, made-up words like 'yeppers' or 'bazillion,' no warnings about things that can ruin your brain cells, no dogs allowed — especially big hairy ones that are named after sandwiches. No bird imitations —"

When she said that, Oggie's eyes got very wide.

"Uh-oh," he said, suddenly looking very worried. "I think we have a problem."

Donnica smiled. It had taken a little longer than anticipated, but her plan was finally working. Oggie Cooder had realized that he would never be able to follow all the rules she had come up with. Ah, sweet victory!

But then something strange happened. Oggie got down on his hands and knees and began crawling around on the floor, frantically lifting up the edges of the rug and peering under the furniture.

"What in the world are you doing?" asked Donnica.

"I'm looking for my Swiss Warbler," Oggie explained. "I must have dropped it when I tripped. I have to find it. I can't do my yellow-bellied sapsucker without it!"

Tweeeeeeet!

Oggie sat up and looked at Donnica.

"What are you looking at me for?" she said. "I didn't make that sound."

He looked at Dawn and Hannah, but they both shook their heads.

Tweeeeeeeeeeeeeeet!

"Oh, no!" cried Oggie when he saw who was making the sound. "What did you do, Turkey Boy?"

Turk, who was sitting by the door, wagged his tail and tried to look innocent, but the

whistling sound coming from his mouth gave him away.

He'd found the Swiss Warbler on the floor and had swallowed it. Now it was stuck in his throat!

Oggie quickly stood up. This was not the first time Turk had eaten something he wasn't supposed to. In fact, it had happened often enough that Oggie already knew the drill.

"I have to go home right away and call the vet, in case I need to bring Turk in to see him," he said.

Donnica was not happy. She was convinced her plan had been about to work, and she wanted to finish what she had begun.

"We have to go over the rest of the rules," she said.

"I don't have time right now," Oggie told her. "I have to call the vet. Besides, I have a terrible memory. Why don't you write down all the rules and bring the list to school with you tomorrow, okay?"

Turk let out another loud *tweeeet!* followed by

about a dozen high-pitched *chirps*, and Oggie hurried off with him.

"Are you sure this plan of yours is going to work?" Dawn asked after Oggie had left. "He seemed a lot more worried about his dog than he did about your party rules."

"Shows what you know," Donnica said with a superior smile.

To be honest, though, a minute earlier Donnica had been feeling worried about the plan, too. But she wasn't as worried anymore. She'd just been handed the secret weapon she'd been searching for — an Oggie-proof rule.

10

The minute Oggie got home, he called the vet and explained what had happened.

"It's probably nothing to worry about," Dr. Roberts told him. "Just feed him a few slices of bread. That ought to knock it loose."

Turk was more than happy to cooperate, but even after he wolfed down four slices of bread, the Swiss Warbler was still stuck in his throat. He didn't seem to be in any pain, and when Oggie checked back with the vet, Dr. Roberts said to give it a little more time and a lot more bread. Oggie decided there was no point in worrying. He decided the same thing about the B.P.R.'s. As long as Donnica brought the list to school in the morning, he'd have enough time to go over it before the party. On

Saturday he would simply bring the list with him in case he needed to refresh his memory about any of the rules.

For years Oggie had sat on his porch steps listening to the laughter and splashing and happy shrieks coming over the high wooden fence that surrounded the Perfectos' swimming pool. He wasn't about to let a few silly rules keep him from finding out how it felt to be on the other side of the fence for a change.

At dinner that night, Oggie told his parents that Donnica had invited him to her birthday party.

"How nice!" said Mrs. Cooder. "The Perfectos have been a lot more friendly lately, have you noticed? Why, just the other day Miriam Perfecto, who never even used to wave when she saw me, practically kissed me when I suggested that all she needed to perk up her begonias was a few handfuls of eggshells."

"Why don't slugs like eggshells?" asked Oggie.

"I suppose they don't like having their tender little bellies scratched," Mrs. Cooder explained.

"I guess that makes you the opposite of a slug, huh, Turkey Boy?" said Oggie, reaching down and giving his dog a quick belly scratch.

Turk rolled over on his back and let out a satisfied *tweeeeeeeeet!*

After helping to clear the dinner table, Oggie went to his room and settled in to finish his homework. He'd already done the math problems and had looked over the spelling words. The only thing he had left to do was to write his haiku. Usually when Oggie had to come up with an idea for a story to write during Creative Writing, he thought about interesting things that had happened to him — like the time he got his toe caught in the bathtub faucet, and his mother had to use a whole stick of butter to make it slippery enough to pull it out. Or the time Turk sat down on a bottle of glue and ended up with his rear end stuck to the carpet.

But Turk's rear end didn't seem like the right kind of thing to write a haiku about, especially since the poem was supposed to be about Oggie. He thought about trying to use the word *prrrrr-ip* in his haiku, but he couldn't decide whether to count it as one syllable or two, so he figured it would be safer not to use it at all. Oggie tried and tried to figure out how to describe the most important thing about himself, his *essence*, but the more he thought about it, the harder it seemed to get.

"What are you working on, son?" asked Mr. Cooder, sticking his head in the doorway to see how Oggie was doing.

"Haiku," said Oggie.

"*Gesundheit!*" said Mr. Cooder.

Oggie laughed at the joke. Haiku *did* sound a lot like *achoo*.

"It's a kind of a poem," Oggie explained. "And I have to write one."

"Sorry, Ogg. I'm not a very poetic guy," said Mr. Cooder. "That's more your mother's department. Want me to send out an S.O.S.?"

"What's an S.O.S.?" Oggie asked.

"That's a signal you send out when you're in trouble. In Morse code it's *dot dot dot dash dash dash dot dot dot*."

Oggie had heard of Morse code. Samuel Morse, the man it was named after, was one of the inventors in the book Oggie had taken out of the library.

"Okay," Oggie told his dad. "Go ahead and send out an S.O.S. I can use all the help I can get."

Mrs. Cooder came in a few minutes later.

"Your father tells me you need a little help with a haiku," she said. "I remember writing those in grade school. What is the pattern again?"

"Five, seven, five," Oggie told her.

"What are you going to write about?" Oggie's mother asked. "Cherry blossoms and mist-covered mountains?"

"No. I'm supposed to write about my essence," Oggie explained, quickly adding, "but not the kind of essence Uncle Vern has in his armpits."

"Thank goodness." Mrs. Cooder laughed. "What have you written so far?"

"Nothing," Oggie confessed. "I'm kind of stuck."

"Sometimes when I'm looking for inspiration, I stand on my head," Mrs. Cooder told him.

"Does it work?" Oggie asked. He had seen his mother stand on her head many times, but had never thought to ask her why.

"It certainly gets the blood circulating," she said. "Why don't you try it and see what happens? Just be careful not to fall over."

After Oggie's mother left, he pulled the pillow off his bed and put it on the floor. But the minute he tried standing on his head, Turk came running over and knocked him down. Turk thought this was a great game, but Oggie had work to do, so after it happened again, Oggie kicked Turk out of the room and closed the door. Then he placed the top of his head in the middle of the pillow and pushed himself up into a headstand.

Turk whined and scratched at the door while Oggie stood on his head and tried to think about his essence. "Who am I?" he asked himself again

and again. His face turned bright red as the blood rushed to his head, but it didn't seem to be helping with the haiku. Then, just as he was about to give up, an idea appeared from out of nowhere, like magic.

"That's it!" Oggie cried as he toppled over onto the carpet.

Ten minutes later Oggie's haiku was not only finished, it was neatly folded and tucked into his backpack ready to bring to school.

11

The next morning, Oggie ran into Donnica, Dawn, and Hannah on their way to school. They were talking about the haiku they'd written for the assignment.

"Mine is totally me," said Donnica proudly. "In other words, *per* —"

Dawn and Hannah hesitated.

"*Per* —" Donnica prompted again.

"— sonal?" Hannah said uncertainly.

"No," said Donnica disgustedly. "Not *personal*. *Perfect*. My haiku is perfect. Perfection is totally my essence."

"I couldn't think of anything at first," Oggie told the girls. "But then I stood on my head. It was kind of like the Heimlich maneuver — you know, that squeezing thing you're supposed to do when some-one's choking? — except instead of a clam shell, a haiku came flying out."

The girls looked at one another.

"Loo —" mouthed Donnica silently to Hannah and Dawn.

"— zer" Hannah and Dawn mouthed back.

"So did you bring the list?" Oggie asked Donnica.

Donnica reached into her backpack and pulled out several sheets of paper, neatly stapled together. "B.P.R." was written in large pink letters across the top of the first page. Before she handed the list to Oggie, Donnica took out a pen and added one more rule.

"'Rule Number One Hundred and One,'" she said as she wrote, "'NO STANDING ON YOUR HEAD ALLOWED.'"

When she finished, she gave the list to Oggie.

"If I were you, I'd stay away from those orange apricots," she told him. "You're going to need all the brain cells you've got if you're going to have these rules memorized by Saturday."

Oggie stopped dead in his tracks.

"Memorized?" he said. "You didn't say anything about memorizing."

"Didn't I?" There was a gleam in Donnica's eyes. "Well, it's right here. See?" Donnica pointed to the last page of her list. "'Rule Number One Hundred, *All* Birthday Party Rules must be memorized.' And you'll have to be able to prove it, too."

"Prove it?" Oggie gulped.

"Yes — I give all my party guests a little quiz before they're even allowed to come in the door. Right, girls?"

Dawn and Hannah nodded like a couple of bobbleheads on a dashboard.

Oggie was pretty sure he could manage to keep from *prrrrr-ip-ing* if he put his mind to it. He could go to the party barefoot instead of wearing shoes or slippers. And it wouldn't be hard to exchange his red bathing suit for another color. But memorizing was another matter. Oggie had trouble memorizing the weekly spelling words, and there were only ten of those. There was absolutely no way he was going to be able to memorize a hundred and one rules by Saturday. Oggie was not going to be able to go to Donnica's birthday party.

And as that disappointing thought entered Oggie's head, something occurred in Wawatosa, Wisconsin, that had never happened before: Donnica Perfecto and Oggie Cooder were thinking the exact same thing.

Kids were already beginning to go inside when Oggie reached the schoolyard. Amy Schneider waved to him from the top of the steps, but he didn't see her. As Oggie walked down the hall toward his classroom, all he could think about was the fun he was going to be missing. What if there were piggies-in-a-blanket? Oggie's aunt Hettie always served those when she had a party. They were delicious little hot dogs rolled up in dough with toothpicks stuck through them. Oggie's uncle

Vern loved them, too, and had once eaten sixty-seven of them in one sitting — including the toothpicks.

Oggie's mouth watered thinking about those piggies-in-a-blanket, but it looked like his imagination was as close as he was going to get to mini–hot dogs now that Donnica had informed him that the rules for her party had to be memorized.

Oggie felt so miserable, Mr. Snolinovsky didn't have to speak to him once about *prrrrr-ip-ing* during class. What was there to *prrrrr-ip* about? A dark cloud hung over Oggie's head all morning, until suddenly, right before lunch, he had a brainstorm. Oggie and Amy sometimes quizzed each other on spelling words. Working together made it much easier. Since Amy was going to Donnica's party, too, maybe they could team up and work together on memorizing the rules!

"I was thinking maybe we should get ready for Donnica's party together," Oggie said the minute Amy sat down at the lunch table.

But Amy got the exact same uncomfortable look

on her face that she'd had the day before when the topic of Donnica's party had come up.

"What's the matter?" Oggie asked.

"Did Donnica really invite you to her party?"

"Yeppers," said Oggie. "I'd show you the invitation, but Turk ate it. He ate my Swiss Warbler, too. I'll tell you about that later. First I want to know if you want to help each other get ready."

"Um. I don't think so," Amy said.

"Why not?"

"Well, for one thing, I'm not going to the party."

"Why not? Don't you like girls either?"

Amy gave him a funny look.

"That's why Dylan isn't going," Oggie explained. "He doesn't like girls. He only likes Ghorks."

Amy gave Oggie an even funnier look.

"*Ghorks?*"

"Yeah," said Oggie, "Ghorks and windowsills. Or something like that. Anyway, how come you're not coming to the party?"

"Because I didn't get invited," said Amy.

"You didn't?" Oggie was genuinely surprised. He had assumed that since Donnica had invited him, she must have invited everybody in the class. "Maybe your invitation got lost in the mail," Oggie said to Amy. "Do you want me to ask Donnica to send you a new one?"

"No," Amy said quickly. "I don't really want to go to Donnica's birthday party. We're not exactly friends, you know."

Oggie felt that dark cloud sliding back into place over his head. If Amy wasn't coming to the party, that meant he was back at square one. He knew he would never be able to memorize all of the rules by himself.

Now it was Amy's turn to ask Oggie what was wrong.

"I was finally going to get a chance to dive into Donnica's pool," Oggie explained sadly, "but now that I can't go to the party, it's probably never going to happen."

"Why can't you go to the party?" Amy asked. "You were invited, weren't you? And you sure seemed excited about it yesterday when you found out about Bumbles."

"I know. But there's no way I'm going to be able to get ready by myself."

"I don't get it," said Amy. "Why do you need help getting ready for a pool party? All you have to do is put on your bathing suit and walk across the street."

"Actually, I can't wear my bathing suit," said Oggie. "It's red. Rule Number Four is no red bathing suits allowed."

"*What?*" said Amy.

"There's a whole list of rules. A hundred and one of them. And I just found out that I have to have them all memorized by Saturday or Donnica says I can't come to the party."

Amy was beginning to get the picture. She hadn't wanted to say anything, but she'd actually been pretty surprised to hear that Oggie had been invited to Donnica's party. It was clear from the way Donnica acted that she didn't like Oggie. So why invite him to the party? Amy was sure there was something fishy going on.

"Where is this list of rules?" she asked.

Oggie pulled Donnica's B.P.R.'s out of his back pocket and handed it across the table to Amy. As Amy began to read, her cheeks turned very pink. She saw right through Donnica's little plan. Obviously Donnica didn't really want Oggie at her party. Tricking him into thinking he had to follow all these rules was just plain mean.

"I can't believe this," Amy said.

"I know," said Oggie. "There's no way I'll ever be able to memorize them all by Saturday."

"Oh, I wouldn't be so sure about that," said Amy.

And suddenly Donnica Perfecto wasn't the only one with a plan.

12

After lunch, Oggie felt a lot better. Amy had promised she would figure out a way to help him get ready for the party. Mr. Snolinovsky collected the homework from the day before. But instead of putting the haiku in his red folder, where he put the rest of the work to be checked, he asked everybody to fold the poems in half and come up one at a time to place each one in a special box he had brought in and placed on the corner of his desk. The box was covered with colorful paper — a background of blue sky decorated with rainbows.

Oggie carefully folded his poem in half, and when it was his turn, he went up and slipped it into the box. Amy came after him, but before she returned to her seat she stopped to admire the pictures on the box.

"I love rainbows," she said.

"Richard of York Gave Battle in Vain," Mr. Snolinovsky replied.

"Pardon?" said Amy politely.

"It's a trick to help you remember the order of the colors in the rainbow," said Mr. Snolinovsky. "I learned it back when I was in grade school and never forgot it. Richard of York Gave Battle in Vain: red, orange, yellow, green, blue, indigo, violet."

"Cool!" said Amy enthusiastically — not because she had learned a new way to remember the colors in the rainbow, but because it had just given her a great idea for how to help Oggie.

During Silent Reading that afternoon, Oggie searched through the book he'd taken out of the library the day before, in hopes of finding the name of the person who had invented the cherry picker. He didn't find what he was looking for, but during his search he did discover that an

American dentist named Edward Angle was the person most people considered responsible for having invented braces. He would have to remember to tell Amy.

As Oggie closed his book and was about to put it away in his desk, Amy happened to walk by. She was on her way to sharpen her pencil in the electric sharpener Mr. Snolinovsky kept on the windowsill, but as she passed Oggie's desk she slowed down and slipped him a note. Oggie unfolded the little triangle of paper and read:

CAN YOU COME OVER THIS AFTERNOON AFTER SCHOOL?

The only plans Oggie had for after school were to do his homework and take Turk for a walk.

"So, can you come?" Amy asked Oggie later as they were walking down the hall together after the last bell.

"Sure, I can. But I have to walk Turk first," Oggie said.

"You can bring him with you, if you want. I'll put Jitters in the laundry room. That way Turk won't try to eat her like last time."

Jitters was Amy's cat, and she made Turk's mouth water the same way Oggie's did when he thought about piggies-in-a-blanket.

"Speaking of eating, should I have a snack before I come over to your house?" Oggie asked. He crossed his fingers and hoped like crazy that Amy would say no. Unlike Oggie's mother, who insisted that Oggie have a healthy snack after school every day — something like raisins or carrot sticks — Amy's mother was not as strict. Oggie was particularly fond of her root beer floats.

"My mom said something about making brownies this afternoon," Amy told Oggie. "And there's always plenty of vanilla ice cream in the freezer if we want to have root beer floats."

Prrrrr-ip! Prrrrr-ip! Oggie (and his sweet tooth) were very happy to hear this news.

"I'll see you in about a half hour, then," said Oggie.

"Okay," said Amy. "Oh, and make sure you bring that list of rules with you when you come."

"Are you sure you don't mind helping me even though you're not invited to the party?" asked Oggie.

"You don't understand," said Amy. "Nothing in the world would give me more pleasure than knowing that you're going to be showing up on Donnica's doorstep on Saturday with all of her silly rules memorized. I'm just sorry I won't be there to see the look on her face."

"I could take a picture," Oggie offered.

Oggie and Amy parted ways and Oggie walked the rest of the way home by himself. He looked for the two Georges, but they must have been working on telephone wires in another neighborhood that day. He would have liked to watch them use the cherry picker again.

Mrs. Cooder was in the kitchen, washing lettuce at the sink when Oggie walked in the door.

"Would you like a snack, Ogg?" she called to him. "I could make you some ants on a log."

Ants on a log = celery sticks with peanut butter and raisins on top. Very healthy.

"No, thanks!" Oggie called back. "I'm going to walk Turk over to Amy's house in a minute. Her mom's making brownies."

"Come here a second first, will you?" said Oggie's mother. "I want to talk to you about something."

Oggie sincerely hoped she wasn't going to try to talk him into eating ants on a log instead of brownies.

Turk, who had been waiting eagerly at the door for Oggie as usual, was prancing around with his leash in his mouth. The Swiss Warbler was still stuck in his throat, but it must have shifted a little because in addition to tweeting and chirping, he could now twitter.

"Just a minute, Turkey Boy," Oggie told him.

Mrs. Cooder put the last of the lettuce in the salad spinner and turned off the water.

"How was school today?" she asked.

"Fine," said Oggie. "I didn't spill my chocolate milk at lunch."

"Did Mr. Snolinovsky like your haiku?"

"Oh, he didn't read it yet. We had to put them all in this box and we're going to do something special with them tomorrow."

"That's nice." Mrs. Cooder walked over to the fridge and dried her hands on the striped dish towel that was hanging from the door handle. "You know, Donnica's birthday party is the day after tomorrow. Some cute little vintage purses came into the store today. Maybe she'd like something like that."

"I don't think I should pick out a present for her until I know for sure whether I'm going to be able to go to the party," said Oggie.

"Why wouldn't you be able to go to the party?" asked Mrs. Cooder.

Oggie pulled the list of rules out of his back pocket and held it out to his mother. But before she could reach for it, Turk jumped up and snatched the

papers away, running out of the room with the list clamped tightly between his sharp teeth.

"Turk! Come back here!" cried Oggie, running after him.

The phone rang and Mrs. Cooder went to answer it while Oggie chased Turk around the couch, diving over the cushions in an attempt to retrieve the papers.

"Excuse me?" said Oggie's mother into the phone. "You'll have to repeat that. I'm afraid we have a bad connection. Who did you say was calling?"

While his mother talked on the phone, Oggie continued to chase Turk, finally managing to corner him and remove the list from his mouth. It was still in one piece, though a bit soggy in places. Turk wriggled free and ran off to find his leash, returning a minute later to drop it at Oggie's feet.

When Oggie made no move to leave, Turk, who was not used to having to wait so long for his afternoon walk, threw back his head and began to howl in frustration. Because of the Swiss Warbler in his throat, the howls came out sounding like *Kweeeeeeeee-urk! Kweeeeeeeee-urk!*

"Hey," cried Oggie, "you sound just like a yellow-bellied sapsucker!"

Turk *Kweeeeeeeee-urk-ed* again, but then Mrs. Cooder put her hand over the phone and called from the kitchen, "Take him outside, will you please, Ogg? I can't hear a thing over all that racket."

So Oggie stuck the list of B.P.R.'s back in his pocket, and he and Turk headed off to Amy's house ... where Oggie hoped a plate of warm brownies would be waiting.

13

Turk was so happy to finally be outside that he took off on a tear, pulling Oggie along behind him like a caboose on a runaway train. As they flew past the entrance to Walnut Acres, Oggie suddenly remembered that he had promised to ask his mom if there were any checked pants left at the store in Dylan's brother's size. Oggie shook his head. Why was it so hard for him to remember things? He sure hoped that Amy was going to be able to help him memorize the B.P.R.'s.

Amy was waiting for Oggie on the front steps when he got there.

"Come here, Turkey Burger," she called, patting her knees with her hands. Turk ran up the steps and began licking her face with his big wet tongue. Amy wrinkled her nose. "Somebody around here could really use a breath mint."

"Who, me?" asked Oggie, cupping a hand over his mouth and sniffing.

Amy giggled.

"I was talking about Turk. Come on in. Jitters is already in the laundry room, so the coast is clear."

Amy's house smelled delicious.

"Hello, Oggie." Mrs. Schneider poked her head around the corner and waved. "Would you like a warm brownie?"

"Does my uncle Vern have eleven toes?" Oggie cried happily.

Mrs. Schneider looked alarmed.

"That's just Oggie's way of saying yes," Amy explained. She knew all about Oggie *and* his uncle Vern's extra toe.

"So did you bring the list?" Amy asked once they'd settled in on the couch in the den with a plate of brownies between them and two big root beer floats with red bendy straws sticking out of the creamy foam.

Oggie pulled the list out of his pocket and, careful to keep it out of Turk's reach this time, handed it to Amy.

"I think I should warn you," Oggie said, "my memory has been worse than ever lately. Do you think it could have anything to do with all those marshmallows I ate the last time we were in Ohio? Uncle Vern was trying to break his record for how many marshmallows he could throw into another person's mouth without missing."

"How many did you eat?" asked Amy.

"Fifty-three. Fifty-four if you count the cotton ball he threw in there by accident."

Amy laughed and took a sip of her root beer float.

"Shall we get started?" she asked.

Oggie groaned and slapped his forehead.

"What's the matter?" Amy asked.

"I just remembered I forgot to bring index cards

so we could make flash cards for the rules like we always do with the spelling words."

"I've got index cards," said Amy.

"One hundred and one of them?" asked Oggie doubtfully.

"We won't need nearly that many," said Amy.

"How come? I have to memorize all the rules, you know."

Amy smiled.

"Richard of York Gave Battle in Vain," she said.

"Who's Richard of York?" asked Oggie, confused. "Is he coming to Donnica's party?"

"No. 'Richard of York Gave Battle in Vain' is a trick for how to remember the order of the colors in the rainbow: red, orange, yellow, green, blue, indigo, violet."

"Neat-o," said Oggie.

"Yeah," said Amy. "And colors aren't the only thing it works for either." She studied the B.P.R.'s for a minute and then put down the list. "Putting Salad Under the Couch Is Very Messy and Danger-ous," she told Oggie.

"Is there really a rule that says you're not allowed to put salad under the couch?" asked Oggie.

"No." Amy laughed. "Each word in the sentence stands for one of the rules. See?" She got a sheet of paper and wrote the letters *P, S, U, T, C, I, V, M, A,* and *D* down the side. Then next to each letter she wrote one of the rules from Donnica's list.

P —NO **PRRRRR-IP-ING**

S — NO CROCHETED **SHOELACES**

U —NO **USED** CLOTHES

T —NO **TRIPPING** OVER YOUR OWN FEET

C —NO **CHARVING**

I —NO TALKING ABOUT **INVENTORS**

V —NO UNCLE **VERN** STORIES

M —NO **MADE-UP** WORDS

A —NO **ANIMAL** IMITATIONS

D —NO **DOGS**

"Oh, I get it!" said Oggie. "This one sentence will help me remember" — he stopped and counted — "ten rules!"

"Now close your eyes and tell me what the sentence was," Amy prompted.

Oggie closed his eyes and rattled it off without a bit of trouble.

"*Putting salad under the couch is very messy and dangerous.* Hey! I remembered!"

Soon enough, he and Amy were pleased to discover that with a little practice, Oggie was also able to remember all ten of the rules the sentence represented.

"I knew it would work!" Amy cried happily. "Now all we have to do is make up funny sentences to help you remember the rest of the rules."

Which is exactly what they did.

That night Oggie went to sleep with a smile on his face. He and Amy had had a great time making up funny sentences to help him remember Donnica's rules. His two favorites were "Some People Enjoy Hot Mustard Ice Cream For Lunch On Wednesdays" and "Fish Don't Fly In Airplanes Unless They Lose Their Bicycles." Of course,

Oggie would still need to spend time going over what all of the letters in the sentences stood for, but things had gone so well with Amy, he was sure that by Saturday he would be ready. He was going to Donnica's party!

On Friday morning, Oggie woke up in a great mood. He walked Turk, grabbed a couple of slices of cheese out of the fridge, and headed off to school. He looked for Amy as soon as he got to the schoolyard, eventually spotting her sitting on a swing, reading a book.

"Can you quiz me?" he asked. "I keep forgetting the NO ANIMAL IMITATIONS rule. I think it's because I don't really do animal imitations, I do birdcalls. At least I used to, before Turk swallowed my Swiss Warbler."

Just then Donnica appeared at the edge of the yard, with Dawn and Hannah at her sides.

"I can't wait to tell Donnica I'm going to be able to come to her party after all," said Oggie. "Hey, Donnica! Guess what?"

But Amy tugged on Oggie's sleeve to hold him back.

"Don't you think it would be more fun if you surprised her?" she said.

"*Prrrrr-ip! Prrrrr-ip!* Good idea," said Oggie.

But Donnica was not the only one who was about to be surprised.

14

As soon as he walked into the classroom, Oggie noticed that the rainbow-covered box was no longer sitting on Mr. Snolinovsky's desk. He also noticed that the bulletin board at the front of the room was completely covered with colored squares of paper that hadn't been there the day before. When he went to have a closer look, Oggie discovered that each piece of paper had three lines typed on it. Haiku!

Oggie searched for his poem, finally locating it on a square of green paper, pinned to the upper right-hand corner of the board.

"There's mine!" he cried happily.

"Don't say another word, Oggie!" Mr. Snolinovsky called from his desk. "Come have a

117

seat so I can explain what we're going to be doing with the haiku."

Once the class was seated and attendance had been taken, Mr. Snolinovsky told everybody that the reason the haiku had been typed up and put on the bulletin board was because they were going to play a game called Whose Haiku Are You?

"As you know, there are no names on the poems, and they have all been typed up so that nobody will be able to guess an author based on his or her penmanship."

"How do you play the game?" asked America.

"You'll have all day today to read the poems and think about who wrote them," Mr. Snolinovsky explained. "This afternoon you'll make your guesses."

"What do we get if we win?" asked David Korben.

"Your reward will be the joy of knowing that you are a thoughtful reader, and that you know your classmates well," Mr. Snolinovsky told him.

"Some prize," grumbled David, who was used to being handed a shiny trophy for his efforts on the basketball court.

Throughout the day, Oggie went and stood in front of the bulletin board, studying the haiku. Some of them were easy to figure out:

Basketball is cool
Cooler than baseball or foot-
Ball or golf. The end.

Although Oggie didn't think it sounded very haiku-ish the way the lines were all choppy and split up, he had to admit it did capture the essence of David Korben, who was clearly the author. Donnica's, as promised, was all about how perfect she was:

How lucky to be
So beautiful and perfect
Don't you envy me?

Bethie Hudson's was about winning a spelling bee — something she never missed an opportunity to remind people she'd done back in the second grade. And there was one other haiku that Oggie felt certain he knew who had written:

Ghorks and Shadow Zwills
How you fill my heart with joy
My secret Ghoulers

It had to be Dylan's. Who else would have written about Ghoulers and Ghorks? Each time Oggie visited the bulletin board, his eyes would drift up to the upper right-hand corner where he would reread his own haiku, wondering whether people would recognize the essence of him in the words.

Many of the haiku were hard to match up with a particular person. There was one about riding a bicycle and another about playing with a cat. Pretty much anybody with a bicycle or a cat could have written those. At noon, before the class was dismissed to go to the cafeteria, Mr. Snolinovsky made everybody promise not to discuss the haiku game during lunch.

"I want your guesses to be based only on the poems," he told them. "Not on hints your friends drop about which ones they wrote."

As promised, Amy and Oggie did not discuss the haiku. Instead, Amy quizzed Oggie on the B.P.R.'s while they ate their sandwiches.

"*'Our moon is not cheese, so what's that funny smell?'*" said Oggie.

"No," Amy corrected. "It's not, '*so* what's that funny smell,' it's '*but* what's that funny smell?' Remember? The *b* stands for brain cells."

"Oh, right," said Oggie. "Rule Number Thirty-Five: NO TALKING ABOUT THE THINGS THAT YOUR PARENTS TELL YOU WILL KILL YOUR **BRAIN CELLS**."

"I wonder why you always forget that one," said Amy.

"Probably those fifty-three marshmallows I ate."

"Or maybe the cotton ball." Amy giggled.

As they walked back to class together after lunch, Oggie asked Amy, "Do you think I'll know all the rules by heart by tomorrow afternoon?"

"Absolutely," Amy told him.

"Well, in that case, do you think Donnica likes purses?"

"That's a weird question," said Amy.

"Not really. If I go to the party, I have to bring a gift. My mom thinks I should give Donnica a purse, but I don't even know if she likes purses."

Amy's personal feeling was that the only thing Donnica Perfecto deserved from Oggie was a big fat punch in the nose.

"If she doesn't like purses, I was thinking maybe I could crochet her some pink shoelaces," said Oggie.

"What about Rule Number Two?" Amy reminded him.

"Do you think it would still be breaking the rule if the shoelaces were in a box?" asked Oggie.

Their conversation was interrupted by a loud voice behind them. Donnica was yelling at her friends.

"How many times do I have to tell you? It's not my fault. I told Daddy that the only thing I wanted for my birthday was Cheddar Jam!"

Oggie's eyes got very wide.

Prrrrr-ip! Prrrrr-ip!

"Did Donnica just say she wanted *cheddar jam* for her birthday?" whispered Oggie excitedly.

"That's what it sounded like to me," Amy confirmed.

"What's cheddar jam?" Oggie asked.

Amy shrugged. Neither she nor Oggie had attended the Valentine Dance, so they hadn't heard of the band. Living in Wawatosa, Wisconsin, though, they were used to people trying to come up with new and creative ways to use cheese. But jam? Oggie squinched up his face as he tried to imagine eating a peanut butter and cheddar jam sandwich. It didn't sound very appetizing.

I wonder why Donnica wants cheese for her birthday, Oggie thought. But it didn't really matter. What was important was that Oggie finally knew what Donnica wanted for her birthday, and he made a promise to himself then and there that he was going to get it for her.

Cheddar jam.

15

That afternoon during Creative Writing, Oggie and his classmates made their final haiku guesses. When they were done, Mr. Snolinovsky took the poems off the board and began to read them aloud. The first one he read was typed on a piece of green paper.

> I do not know yet
> Exactly what it will be
> But you will need it.

Amy was the only one who guessed correctly that Oggie had written it. She knew all about Oggie's dreams of being an inventor. Oggie had guessed right about Donnica's and David's and

Bethie's haiku, but to his surprise, Dylan turned out to be the person who had written about the bicycle.

So who wrote the haiku about Ghoulers and Ghorks? Oggie wondered. When Mr. Snolinovsky got to that one and asked the author to stand, Oggie couldn't have been more surprised. But he was not as surprised as the person sitting in the first seat in the third row.

"You collect Ghoulers?!" Dylan cried in utter amazement.

Dylan James had seen the poem on the board and had been waiting on the edge of his seat all day to find out who had written it. Imagine how shocked he was to discover that the one person at Truman who liked the same thing he did was . . . Amy Schneider. *A girl.*

After school that day, Oggie went to three grocery stores and two cheese shops. He saw cheddar balls, cheddar wheels, cheddar straws, cheddar sticks, and cheddar you could squirt right out of a can. But nobody had heard of cheddar jam. Discouraged, he decided to swing by Too Good to Be Threw and ask for his mother's advice.

"Why do you want to give Donnica jelly for her birthday?" asked Mrs. Cooder.

"Jam," Oggie corrected.

"Are you sure she wouldn't rather have a purse?"

But Donnica had said she wanted cheddar jam. There was one more place Oggie hadn't tried. As he headed out the door to continue his search, a flash of yellow and blue caught his eye and he snapped his fingers as he remembered Dylan's brother's request. A few minutes later, Oggie was walking down the street with a pair of blue-and-yellow-checked pants in Justin's size tucked under his arm.

On his way home, Oggie stopped at the mini-mart attached to the Gas and Go filling station. It was his last hope, but it turned out that the only kind of cheese they had was plain old American, and even that looked a little moldy. Oggie kept his eyes peeled for the Georges and the cherry picker as he continued on his way, but again it seemed they were nowhere in sight. Turk was waiting by the door with his leash in his mouth when Oggie got home, so he dropped his backpack on the kitchen table, hooked the leash on Turk's collar, and the two of them started off toward Walnut Acres to deliver the pants to Dylan's brother.

As he walked his dog, Oggie resigned himself to the fact that he wasn't going to be able to give Donnica what she really wanted for her birthday. He was disappointed, but what could he do? He'd looked everywhere he could think of for cheddar jam, but it was nowhere to be found.

Nobody was home at the Jameses' house. Dylan's bike was gone and there was no car in the driveway. The red trunk was still sitting on the lawn, so Oggie sat down on it and waited for a while to see if anybody showed up. After about ten minutes, he gave up. Before he left, he folded the pants and left them sitting on top of the trunk where he hoped Justin would find them.

That night before he went to bed, Oggie crocheted Donnica a pair of pink shoelaces. He used a ruler to make sure they were both exactly the same length. Maybe he hadn't been able to find cheddar jam, but at least Oggie could make sure that Donnica wouldn't be tripping over uneven shoelaces.

The next morning Oggie awoke feeling nervous and excited. In just a few hours he would be swimming in Donnica Perfecto's pool! He got up and tried to make himself a bowl of cereal, but he was so worked up, first he spilled the last of the cornflakes on the floor and then he knocked over the milk carton. Turk was delighted, and more than happy to help with the cleanup. Oggie had really been too excited to eat breakfast anyway. He looked at the clock. It was only eight fifteen. How was he ever going to last until party time?

At nine o'clock, Oggie put Donnica's shoelaces in a box and carefully tied a ribbon around it. At ten o'clock Mrs. Cooder drove Oggie down to Selznick's department store, where they exchanged his red bathing suit for a yellow one. Oggie also talked his mother into buying him a pair of rubber swim fins he discovered in the sale bin. There was no rule against swim fins on Donnica's list, and Oggie could hardly wait to try them out in the Perfectos' pool. At eleven o'clock, Amy called to quiz Oggie one last time on the rules and to wish him good luck.

"Thanks a BAZILLION for all your help," Oggie told her. "And by the way, how come you never told me you collected Ghorks and Windowsills?"

"They're called *Shadow Zwills*," Amy told him. "And I didn't tell you because I didn't think you'd be interested since you can't play Old Maid with them."

She knew Oggie well.

At twelve o'clock, Oggie was too excited to eat lunch, so he went to his room and *prrrrr-ip-ed* non-stop for an hour and a half. When he was finished, his tongue was completely numb. He tested himself by thinking about piggies-in-a-blanket and he was very relieved to find that he had *prrrrr-ip-ed* himself dry.

It felt like two o'clock would never come, but at last it did. Oggie put on his new bathing suit and got Turk settled in the backyard with a bone to chew on to keep him busy while he was gone. Before he left the house, without even thinking about it, Oggie stopped at the fridge, took out a few slices of American cheese, and slipped them into one of the pockets of his swim trunks.

As Oggie was leaving the house in his bathing suit and swim fins, a familiar white truck came cruising up Tullahoma Street. When it stopped in front of the Cooders' house, Oggie was delighted to see who it was.

"Hi, Georges!" Oggie called to his friends from the phone company. "What are you doing here?"

The two Georges were glad to see Oggie. They explained that they were in the neighborhood because there had been some trouble reported with the phone lines. Oggie remembered that his mother had mentioned something about bad reception only the day before.

"Looks like you're on your way to a party," one of the Georges said, noticing the box with the bow on it in Oggie's hand.

"Yeppers!" said Oggie happily. "It's a swim party and there might even be piggies-in-a-blanket."

"Have fun," they told Oggie. Then Short George climbed into the bucket and Tall George began to raise him up to the phone lines.

As Oggie started flip-flopping across the street in his swim fins, a green van with a watering can painted on the side pulled into the Perfectos' driveway. Several women wearing straw hats climbed out. Oggie waved to them, figuring they were probably relatives of Donnica's who had come to help celebrate her birthday. When Oggie reached the front door, he rang the bell. After a minute, Mrs. Perfecto answered the door.

"Hello," said Oggie, holding out the present to her. "Thank you for inviting me. Here's a gift for Donnica. I made them myself."

But instead of inviting him to come inside, Mrs. Perfecto gasped and put her hands on her cheeks.

"Oh no," she whimpered miserably. "Not now. Not today."

For a minute Oggie thought he must have gotten the day of the party mixed up, but then he noticed that Mrs. Perfecto was looking past him at the ladies in the straw hats. Mrs. Perfecto pushed Oggie out of the way and hurried down the walk, leaving Oggie to show himself into the house.

"Hello?" he called. "Anybody here?"

"Everybody's out back by the pool," came a muffled reply.

At first Oggie didn't see him, because the owner of the voice was sitting on the couch, which happened to be the exact same shade of brown as the fur suit he was wearing.

"Bumbles!" cried Oggie.

The giant bear lifted a paw and waved.

"What are you doing in here?" Oggie asked. "Shouldn't you be outside juggling by the pool?"

"The birthday girl told me to stay inside," said Bumbles. "And it's a good thing, too, because the cleaner shrank my suit and now the eyeholes are in the wrong place. I can't see a thing."

They were interrupted by the sound of a gasp coming from the other end of the room. Donnica, in a pink bathing suit with a terry cloth robe on over it, was standing in the doorway, staring at Oggie as if she were seeing a ghost.

"What are you doing here?" she said.

"You invited me to your party," Oggie told her. "Remember?"

"Of course I remember," she said, "but you told me you had a terrible memory so you couldn't possibly come. *Remember?*"

"I *do* have a terrible memory," Oggie said. "But Amy Schneider and Richard of York helped me, and I memorized every single rule. Want to hear? 'Putting salad under the couch is very messy and dangerous.' Which means no *prrrrr-ip-ing*, no crocheted shoelaces, no Uncle Vern stories . . ."

But Donnica wasn't listening. Her mind was racing a million miles an hour. Oggie Cooder and Bumbles the Bear were both at her birthday party. If she didn't want to be the laughingstock of the entire fourth grade, she needed a new plan and she needed it fast.

16

Donnica wasted no time launching Plan B.

"Quick, you two," she told Oggie and Bumbles. "Follow me. Dawn is upstairs stuck in the bathroom, and you have to help rescue her."

"Rescue Dawn?" asked Oggie.

"Yes," said Donnica. "The bathroom door gets stuck sometimes and the only way to get it open is to push it from the outside. You both have to come rescue her."

"You want me to come, too?" asked Bumbles.

"Uh, *duh*, Yogi," said Donnica. "I said I need both of you, didn't I?"

There was a loud crash as Bumbles stood up, accidentally knocking over a lamp.

"Sorry," he said, trying to pick up the lamp and

in the process knocking a stack of magazines off the coffee table and onto the floor. "I really can't see a thing. I'd take my head off, but I think the zipper's jammed."

"Forget about your head. There's no time for that now. We have to get upstairs!" shouted Donnica.

Oggie tossed the birthday present on the table and grabbed Bumbles by the paw. Together, the two of them stumbled up the stairs behind Donnica.

"Okay," Donnica said when they reached the top of the stairs. "Here's what we're going to do. You two lean against this door, and on the count of three push as hard as you can."

Oggie and Bumbles did as they were told and put their shoulders to the door.

"Ready?" said Donnica. "One . . . two . . . three!"

The minute they leaned against the door, it flew open and Bumbles and Oggie tumbled into the bathroom, landing in a tangle together on the floor.

Knowing she didn't have a second to spare, Donnica pulled the door shut, and using the belt from her robe, she quickly tied the outside bathroom doorknob to the knob on the door of the linen closet right next to it in the hall.

Bumbles and Oggie were trapped in the bathroom!

"What's going on?" Oggie asked as he jiggled the knob in vain.

"Oops!" Donnica yelled through the door. "I guess Dawn wasn't locked in there after all. But now you guys are. Don't worry, though — - I'll go find someone to help get you out. I'll be right back."

But Donnica had no intention of coming back. Plan B had worked perfectly. She had Oggie Cooder and Bumbles exactly where she wanted them.

Bumbles and Oggie waited for half an hour for Donnica to return. When she didn't come back, they tried pounding on the door, but everybody was outside in the backyard, and Donnica had turned the music up loud so nobody would be able to hear them.

"I had a bad feeling about this gig from the beginning," groaned Bumbles. "But I need the money. Now I probably won't even get paid."

Oggie climbed up on the edge of the bathtub so he could look out of the window. The green van was still parked in the driveway, but there was no sign of Mrs. Perfecto or the ladies in the straw hats. Across the street, the two Georges were working on the phone wires. Oggie cranked open the window as far as it would go and called out to them, but they couldn't hear him over the loud music that was playing out by the pool, where the party was now in full swing. Oggie sniffed the air and was certain he smelled piggies-in-a-blanket.

"What are we going to do?" Oggie asked.

"I don't know," said Bumbles, "but I'll tell you one thing — if I don't get out of this suit soon, I'm going to burn up. You wouldn't believe how hot it is in here."

Oggie went around behind Bumbles and tried to get the zipper on the bear suit unstuck, but it was no use. It was completely jammed.

"Maybe we should cut the legs off so you can take the suit off from the bottom instead," Oggie suggested.

"Go for it," came Bumbles's muffled reply.

So Oggie found a pair of toenail clippers in the medicine cabinet and began to cut the suit apart. As he clipped away at the brown fur, a familiar flash of yellow and blue caught his eye.

"Hey!" said Oggie. "Where'd you get those pants?"

A few minutes later when Bumbles finally managed to wriggle out of his bear suit, Oggie had his answer: Bumbles the Juggling Bear was none other than Dylan's brother, Justin James.

"Hey, Oggie," said Justin, brushing his long hair out of his eyes and tucking it behind his ears. "I didn't realize it was you out here."

"I didn't realize it was you in there either," said Oggie. "Are you really Bumbles the Bear?"

"The one and only," said Justin. "And it looks like now I owe you two favors. One for the pants and one for getting me out of my costume. Thanks, man. I was really roasting in there. I wish someone would come up with a way to air-condition a bear suit."

Justin reached over and picked up four seashell-shaped soaps that were sitting in a dish next to the sink. At first Oggie thought he was planning to wash his hands, but instead Justin tossed the soaps up in the air and began to juggle them.

"Neat-o!" said Oggie. "I wish I could do that."

"It's easy once you get the hang of it," Justin told him. "I could teach you."

"*Prrrrr-ip! Prrrrr-ip!*" went Oggie.

"Are you okay?" asked Justin, who had never heard anybody make that sound before. "Do you need a drink of water or something?"

"I'm fine," said Oggie. "I just *prrrrr-ip* sometimes when I'm excited. Yellow-bellied sapsuckers

do the same thing — only they say *k-waan k-waan*."

Justin laughed and handed Oggie one of the soaps.

"Okay. Start by tossing this back and forth, from your right hand to your left, until you get the feel of it," he said.

At first Oggie threw the soap too high and too fast, but then Justin explained that it should travel in a slow arc through the air from one hand to the other. Once Oggie could do that, Justin handed him another soap.

"Start with both of them in the same hand," he instructed. "Then throw one and hang on to the other."

This proved to be more difficult to do than it sounded. Oggie tried to throw only one soap at a time, but no matter how hard he tried, he couldn't seem to keep the second soap from slipping out along with the first. Both soaps would fly out in different directions, making it impossible to catch either one. Finally, when one of the runaway soaps went flying at the mirror hard enough to break it, Justin reached out and grabbed it just in the nick of time. The juggling lesson was over.

"Maybe I can teach you later, after we get out of here," Justin said. "Speaking of getting out of here, what do you think is taking so long?"

"I don't know," Oggie said. "Donnica said she'd be right back. You don't think she forgot about us, do you?"

"She better not have," Justin said. "'Cause if I'm not ready to go when the guys get here to pick me up I'm going to be in big trouble. We've got a practice this afternoon."

"We may have to get out of here on our own," said Oggie.

"Got any ideas?" Justin asked him.

Oggie thought for a minute and then he snapped his fingers. Actually, he did have an idea!

17

"How about we cut the elastic out of our underwear and use it to shoot the soaps out the window like my uncle Vern did with his mini-pumpkins?" Oggie suggested. "Somebody will find soap out on the front lawn and figure out we're trapped up here."

"Uh, that sounds kind of weird," said Justin. "Let's see if we can think of a plan that doesn't involve cutting up our underwear, okay?"

Oggie looked around and spotted a basket of wire hair curlers sitting on the counter. He snapped his fingers again.

"These are kind of like the wagon springs Elisha Otis used for his elevator brakes. We could tie them to our feet and jump out the window."

"Uh, that sounds kind of dangerous," Justin pointed out. "And besides, I don't think we can fit through that window. It doesn't open wide enough."

Oggie looked around again. This time his gaze settled on the head of Justin's bear costume.

"*Prrrrr-ip Prrrrr-ip!*" went Oggie.

"Got something good?" asked Justin hopefully.

"Do I ever!" said Oggie. "I just thought of a great invention."

"Will it get us out of this bathroom?" asked Justin.

"Nope, but it will keep you cool inside your bear head." Oggie explained to Justin how his invention would work.

"See, there will be a little fan — the kind that runs on batteries — and an ice bag to lower the temperature of the air. Then you'll have this big rubber band to attach it to your head and, presto, instant air-conditioning!"

Justin grinned.

"That's brilliant, little dude. You should call it

the Cooder Fan. How did you come up with that idea anyway?"

"Necessity is the mother of invention," said Oggie happily.

Justin looked nervously at his watch. "The guys are going to be here any minute. Anybody who could come up with something as great as the Cooder Fan ought to be able to think of a way to get us out of here. Come on, Oggie, *concentrate*."

The last time Oggie had needed to concentrate on something was when he'd been trying to come up with an idea for his haiku. He knew what he had to do.

"Hey, this is no time to be taking a nap," Justin said as Oggie got down on the floor and started folding up the bath mat to make a pillow.

"I'm not taking a nap," said Oggie. He placed the top of his head on the bath mat and pushed himself up into a headstand.

"Trust me," said Oggie. "This is going to work."

And sure enough, it did. Because no sooner

had Oggie turned upside down than a solution to the problem came flying out — of his pocket.

Oggie had forgotten all about the cheese he had slipped into the pocket of his swimsuit.

"Mmmm," said Justin, picking up a slice of cheese and beginning to pull the wrapper off. "I could really use a snack."

"Wait!" cried Oggie as Justin lifted the cheese to his mouth. "Don't bite that!"

"Why not?" asked Justin.

"That cheese is our ticket out of here!" Oggie proclaimed.

As Justin watched in amazement, Oggie began to charve, tilting his head as he went around the curves and picking up speed until he was nibbling so fast his teeth were a blur.

When he had finished, there were three perfectly charved orange letters in Oggie's lap. Two curvy S's and a big round O.

"What are we going to do with those?" asked Justin.

"We're going to send out an S.O.S.," Oggie explained. Then he carried the letters over to the window and carefully stuck them backward onto the glass so the message would read correctly from the outside.

Justin was very impressed.

"Like I said, you are one clever little dude, Oggie Cooder. If this works, I'm going to owe you big-time."

Those words were barely out of Justin's mouth when there was a tap on the window.

"You boys need a lift?"

It was one of the Georges. He'd looked across the street and seen Oggie's cheesy S.O.S. stuck to the window and had immediately told the other George to use the controls to send the bucket of the cherry picker over to investigate. Using a screwdriver, he managed to remove the window from the outside, and in no time at all the two boys were clambering into the bucket.

"Oops. Almost forgot something," said Justin,

and he quickly slipped back inside to retrieve his bear suit.

"*Prrrrr-ip! Prrrrr-ip!*" went Oggie as the bucket began to go down.

"You can say that again," Justin said, laughing.

"Okay," said Oggie, and he *prrrrr-ip-ed* again.

The commotion out in the front yard attracted the attention of Donnica's party guests. Pretty soon they were all gathered around the truck watching the rescue.

"Okay, everybody," said Short George as he pulled open the door on the side of the bucket. "Show's over. You boys hop out, and the rest of you move back so we can get this truck out of here."

Donnica, who had just sat down to open her birthday gifts when the excitement began, was furious.

"I will never forgive you for this, Oggie Cooder!" she screamed. "How dare you ruin my birthday party!"

But Donnica's hissy fit was interrupted when Hannah Hummerman suddenly put her hand up to her forehead and began to sway back and forth.

"L-l-l-look!" she said, pointing at Justin with a trembling finger. "It's J.J.!!!"

18

It takes a long time and a lot of hard work to save up enough money to buy yourself a car. But that's exactly what Justin James was trying to do, which is why he bussed tables at the Clam Digger and juggled bowling pins at birthday parties in an overheated bear suit and every now and then showed up at a bar mitzvah or a store promotion or a school dance to play in a rock band called Cheddar Jam.

Hannah Hummerman had been the first to recognize J.J. as he climbed out of the cherry picker in his blue-and-yellow-checked pants, brushing his long blond hair out of his eyes. Soon, all the other girls (and even some of the boys) were going crazy, too. Things got wilder when a beat-up van plastered with bumper stickers pulled up to the curb, carrying the rest of the guys in the band.

"Come on, J.J.," one of them called. "Time to rock and roll."

"Cheddar Jam! Cheddar Jam! Cheddar Jam!" the kids started chanting.

Donnica just stood there in her bathing suit with her mouth hanging open.

The boys in the band, enjoying the attention, got out of the van and began to sign autographs on the birthday napkins and scraps of paper thrust into their hands by their starstruck fans.

"I can't believe I didn't faint when I realized that was J.J.," Hannah said to Dawn. "I one-hundred-percent guarantee I almost fainted."

Of course, Oggie was surprised to learn that Cheddar Jam wasn't something you spread on bread. No wonder he hadn't been able to find it at the Gas and Go! But even in all the excitement of being locked in the bathroom and rescued by the cherry picker, Oggie hadn't forgotten the promise he'd made to himself.

"Thanks a million, Mr. P," Justin said to Donnica's father as he tossed his tattered bear suit into the red trunk he used to transport his costume and juggling equipment. "This extra cash is really going to come in handy."

Mr. Perfecto felt so bad about what had happened, he'd paid Justin double for the party, even though the only thing he'd juggled that afternoon was the soap in the upstairs bathroom.

"See you later, Oggie!" Justin called as he closed the lid of the trunk and began to lug it over to the van. "Stop by the house any time and I'll give you another juggling lesson, okay?"

Justin slid open the door, and as he and the rest of the guys started to pile in, Oggie knew it was now or never.

"Wait!" he cried.

"What's the matter?" asked Justin.

"I need to cash in those favors," Oggie told him.

Then he took a deep breath and dove in. "See, I never got invited to one of Donnica's parties before, so I wanted to give her something she really, really, really wanted, and when I found out what she really, really, really wanted was cheese jelly, I looked for it everywhere, but I couldn't find it 'cause cheese jelly doesn't even exist, but now that I know that it wasn't really cheese jelly she wanted —"

"Oggie?" Justin interrupted. "I kind of have to get going. Do you think we could talk about this favor you need a little later?"

"Not really," said Oggie. "See, I was wondering if maybe you and your band could play at Donnica's party."

Donnica, Dawn, and Hannah had been listening to this conversation, and when Oggie got to his point, they gasped in perfect unison. Hannah put her hand up to her forehead as if she were going to faint.

"You mean right now?" asked Justin.

Oggie nodded.

Justin had a short powwow with his bandmates in the van and managed to convince them that they could just as easily practice next to the Perfectos' pool as they could in the garage where they usually rehearsed.

When the guys started unpacking the drums and guitars and amplifiers from the back of the van, the crowd of party guests realized what was happening and took up a new chant.

"Og-gie! Og-gie! Og-gie!"

Cheddar Jam set up and plugged in. When they were ready to play, Justin grabbed the microphone and announced —

"This first song goes out to a cool little dude named — Oggie Cooder."

Everybody clapped and whooped. Oggie would have *prrrrr-ip-ed*, but his mouth was too full of piggies-in-a-blanket.

That afternoon Cheddar Jam played every song they knew (some of them more than once), while Donnica's party guests danced and clapped. All Oggie wanted to do was paddle around in the pool, but girls kept asking him to dance, so he'd hop out of the water, dance around in his swim fins for a few minutes, and then dive back in. Oggie was having fun, but he kept wishing that Amy was there, too. Without her help, he would never have gotten to go to the party.

"More piggies-in-a-blanket on the way, you little party animal you!" Mrs. Perfecto called out to Oggie. Her tone of voice was genuinely friendly now. She was in a terrific mood. Not only was her daughter having the best birthday of her life, but Mrs. Perfecto had been invited to join the garden club. In truth, the ladies in the straw hats had been much more impressed with the landscaping across the street at the Cooders' house, but Isabel Cooder had told them that Miriam Perfecto had taught her everything she knew about gardening and that they would be foolish not to snap her up for their club.

"Pssst! Oggie! Over here."

Oggie looked around, finally catching sight of Amy's head poking over the top of the fence. He was so happy to see her, he jumped out of the pool and ran right over.

"I was just thinking about you," he said.

"We came to see how the party was going," said Amy.

"*We?*" Oggie asked.

Suddenly Amy's head started to wobble. Then she started to giggle.

"Dylan's holding me up," she said. "At least he's trying to."

"Hi, Oggie," called Dylan. "How's it going?"

"Good," Oggie called back. "Hey, did you know your brother is Bumbles the Bear and that he's in a band called Cheddar Jam?"

"Of course I knew." Dylan laughed. "He's my brother, isn't he?"

"So what are you guys up to?" Oggie asked. As fun as it was to be swimming in the pool, he realized he kind of wished he could be hanging out with Amy and Dylan instead.

"We're not doing much. Just talking about Ghorks and junk," said Amy. Her head started to wobble again and this time Dylan must have lost his grip because suddenly Amy disappeared completely. Oggie heard the two of them laughing.

"Um, Oggie?"

Oggie turned around and there was Donnica, holding the pink shoelaces in her hand.

"I just wanted to thank you," she said. "For the present."

"You're welcome. I hope you like them," said Oggie. "I was going to give you an old purse, but I decided you might like some pink shoelaces better and I promised myself that no matter what, I was going to give you something that you really, really *really* —"

"The shoelaces are great," Donnica interrupted. "Really. In fact, they're the *nicest* shoelaces I've ever seen. Which is why you'll probably never see me wear them. I wouldn't want to risk ruining something so, um, *unique*."

Oggie smiled.

"Don't worry, Donnica. If you wreck 'em, I can always make you another pair," he said.

"No, no. That's okay," Donnica said quickly.

"One pair is plenty. But really, I just wanted to say thanks, you know, not just for the shoelaces, but also for getting the band to play at my party. That was really nice of you."

Donnica turned to leave, but suddenly Amy piped up from behind the fence.

"Not so fast, Perfecto. Don't you have something else you want to tell Oggie?"

Donnica blushed her favorite shade of pink — bubblegum.

"I'm sorry I locked you in the bathroom, Oggie," she said, hanging her head.

"And?" Amy prompted.

"I'm sorry I made up all those silly rules," Donnica told Oggie.

"And?" said Amy.

Donnica paused for a minute, puzzled.

"What else did I do?" she asked.

"I don't know," said Amy. "But knowing you, I'm sure there's more."

Oggie stayed at the party long enough to sing "Happy Birthday" to Donnica and to eat a piece of cake. He asked Mrs. Perfecto to wrap up two slices to bring to the Georges to thank them for coming to the rescue with their cherry picker. When he got home he was delighted to find Amy and Dylan waiting for him on the porch steps.

"Guess what we figured out?" said Dylan. "You can play Old Maid with Ghouler cards!"

"Yeah," said Amy. "You just have to use a Shadow Zwill for the Old Maid."

"Neat-o!" said Oggie.

They were interrupted by a strange sound coming from the Cooders' backyard.

"*KWEE-URK! Kwee-urk! Week-week wurp-wurp!*"

"What's that?" asked Dylan, alarmed.

Oggie grinned.

"It's a yellow-bellied sapsucker," he told Dylan.

"Yeah." Amy giggled. "A big fat furry one with bad breath."

(Five days later, Turk would surprise everyone by winning first place in the Wawatosa birdcalling contest. It would be the last time he would

compete, however, because when Oggie gave him a big hug to congratulate him, the Swiss Warbler came flying out of Turk's mouth like a rocket.)

That afternoon, after Oggie and his friends had finished playing a few rounds of Ghouler Old Maid out on the porch, Amy suggested that they turn the sprinkler on and run through it to cool off. Even Turk joined in. Next door, Donnica's party was still in full swing. Oggie was glad that she had liked her shoelaces, and that he'd managed to get her Cheddar Jam, even if it was by accident. He had enjoyed finally getting to swim in the Perfectos' beautiful kidney-shaped pool (not to mention all those piggies-in-a-blanket he'd gotten to eat). But that wasn't the reason he threw back his head and let out a loud *prrrrr-ip prrrrr-ip!*

Oggie Cooder was glad to be back on his side of the fence with his friends and his dog and the bazillion other things that made him feel really, really, *really* happy.

SARAH WEEKS went to many, many parties in order to research this book. She was even invited to a few of them! When she hasn't been party-crashing, she's managed to write many widely acclaimed books, including *So B. It*, the Guy series (*Regular Guy*, *Guy Time*, *My Guy*, and *Guy Wire*), and the Boyds Will Be Boyds series (*Beware of Mad Dog*; *Get Well Soon, Or Else!*; *Danger! Boys Dancing*; and *Fink's Funk*). This is her second Oggie Cooder book. She lives in New York City, and can be found on the Web at www.sarahweeks.com.

NO CHEESE WAS HARMED IN
THE MAKING OF THIS BOOK.